Bad Girls Don't Die

an Al Pennyback mystery

Charles Ray

Uhuru Press
North Potomac, MD

This is a work of fiction, and is not meant to represent any place, event, or person, and where the real thing is mentioned, it is in a fictionalized form only. Any similarities to real places, events or persons (living or dead) is purely coincidental.

For information about this and other works of this author, contact the author at charlesray.author@gmail.com.

Printed in the United States of America

Cover design by the author.

Charles Ray

Chapter 1

The first thing she noticed was the darkness. It wasn't the dark, just able to make out vague shapes kind of darkness, but the stygian, can't see your hand in front of your face kind of darkness. For a heartbeat, it frightened her, really, really frightened.

Was she dead, she wondered? Is this what death is; a great darkness, cut off from everything, a nothingness? If so, then hell, which is where she thought she surely was, was not the place of eternal fire as her grandfather had often threatened, but was, instead, a place of aloneness, a place of dark silence, which, she concluded rather quickly, was infinitely worse than being consigned to the fire along with all the other sinners—the bad people like her. At least, in the fiery pits, she could see others who were suffering the same fate. Here, alone in the darkness, she faced eternity the same way she had come into the world, alone and stripped bare.

All of this took place in a single heartbeat. Just enough time for her to know that she was not dead. At least, not yet.

And, after that single heartbeat, the oppressive darkness began to lift. As the irises of her eyes, which had for some reason contracted to pinpoints, began to open, the darkness was no longer so . . . dark. In fact, she began to be able to make out vague shapes. A light-grey rectangle high above her that might be a window of some sort, but it was either covered by a thin cloth, or painted over. Long, narrow rectangles that in time resolved themselves into wooden beams interlocked in a pattern of large squares above her head, and receding into the murky darkness in the distance. From this pattern, other beams ran straight down, ending at a grayish, dusty looking surface.

Somewhere in the murkiness she heard the 'drip', 'ting,' 'rumble' of water flowing through old and corroded pipes.

Piece by piece, her mind began to assemble what her eyes were seeing and her ears were hearing into a semblance of reality that she could comprehend. The beams were the supporting framework of a floor, with load-bearing beams, that indicated she was in a basement, and from her inability to see a far wall—she could feel the rasp of wallboard at her back—a rather large basement.

This was familiar. She'd spent a lot of time in basements in her life, or in what passed for a life since the untimely death of her parents when she was eleven years old. A basement was where she'd often been sent when she'd been 'bad,' which was most of the time.

She tried moving, and found that she couldn't move her hands apart. She could, however, bend them, so she did. Holding them near her eyes, she could just make out the silvery color of duct tape, several layers of it wrapped tightly around her wrists, pinning them together. She tried moving her legs, and was rewarded with a clanking sound, and the rough scraping of something hard against her ankles.

Well now, this is new. Never before when she'd been sent to the basement had she been shackled. Sure, the door to the ground floor had been locked, but she'd had free run of the place.

Had she been really so bad this time? Had she done something to merit this extra punishment? In that heartbeat of time it had taken her brain to determine her location, it had not determined the why. A significant piece was missing.

Why am I here?

Then, as her vision became clearer, she realized that this was not the basement with which she was familiar. This was a place she'd never been before.

Where am I?

As her heart rate, which had been she now realized, as fast and loud as a kettle drum, slowed, and her breathing, which had been a rapid panting, returned to something approaching normal, her thoughts began to clear, and they weren't comforting.

Is this where I'm supposed to die? Am I now to pay the price for the bad thing I did? What did I do?

She found that the thought of dying did not itself trouble her as much as dying alone in this dark place, to lie undiscovered for who knows how long. Would she be found some day, when she was nothing but a pile of yellowing bones, or would she be buried and forgotten, never to be found, when at some point in the future the structure above the basement collapsed into a pile of rubble, or was demolished and covered by some new construction. That thought bothered her.

I will not be forgotten. I will not die here.

Charles Ray

Chapter 2

Buster and I were having a late lunch at Mom's, a Friday tradition we'd recently established, but that we missed about every other week because one or the other of us was tied up with a case. I was having meat loaf with mashed potatoes and gravy, with four of Mom's famous buttermilk biscuits on a saucer at the side of my plate, while he was attacking a pile of golden fried chicken, sweet corn, baked beans, and corn muffins. We were both drinking iced tea, mine unsweetened, his with so much sugar in it I could see the prisms of light refracted in the amber color.

Buster is Buster Mayweather, a detective lieutenant with the District of Columbia Metro Police, and one of my oldest friends, and Mom's is . . . just Mom's; a soul food diner that has been a presence on Sixteenth Street near U Street, in the renovated U Street corridor of Northwest DC, since Buster and I were still messing our diapers.

And, I am Al Pennyback, Albert Einstein Pennyback on my birth certificate, thanks to a mother who had a thing for the German scientist, and a dream that one day I would follow in his footsteps—I disappointed her by joining the army right after I graduated from high school—but, people who know me know better than to use my full name. To them, I'm just Al. To strangers, I'm Mr. Pennyback. I'm a private detective. I run a two-person shop on Fourth Street, just north of Fort Lesley J. McNair in the District's Southwest section, where my partner, Heather Bunche, and I provide investigative services to people who can't get help from the system, when we're not serving papers or tracking down deadbeat clients on behalf of Holcombe, Stein and Chang, the law firm that has us on a ten thousand dollar per month retainer, thanks to the efforts of my other best friend, Quincy Chang, a colleague from my army days at Fort Bragg, North Carolina, where I served in a special unit attached to Delta Force, and he was a Judge Advocate General officer serving in the JAG office at post headquarters.

When you add Sandra Winter, my girlfriend of long-standing, and Carlton 'Blood' Raine, an octogenarian former CIA field agent, you have the only five people on my list of friends—well, I guess you also have to add Buster's wife, Alma, and his twins, Albert and Sandra, for whom Sandra and I are godparents. Not, mind you, that I'm an unfriendly person, but I have high standards, and they're the only people who make the cut.

I have a few people who aren't exactly friends, but are people I'm willing to talk to, so you can see I'm not a total recluse. In fact, I'm actually a quite nice person when you get to know me.

I watched Buster demolish several drumsticks, including biting off the knobby ends of the bones, chewing, and swallowing—to get at the marrow, he says. The amazing thing is, eating as much as fast as he does, he never seems to get indigestion. In fact, sometimes he seems like an alligator, swallowing his food whole rather than chewing it.

"What's on your mind, bro?" he asked, snapping me out of my reverie.

I hadn't realized that I was sitting there with my fork of meat loaf halfway to my mouth, looking through the plate glass window at the street beyond.

"Nothing," I said, which was mostly true. It was nothing that needed to be the topic of conversation. "Just bored is all. Heather and I haven't had a decent case for months, and I'm tired of sitting in my office looking at the cracks in the ceiling."

It didn't help that it was a Friday near the middle of September, and the weather was perfect. There are two times in the DC area when the weather is actually livable, mid-April to mid-May, and mid-September to mid-October. Except for the pollen, the spring is almost perfect, with bright flowers, moderate temperatures, and the beginning of short dresses on the Mall, while fall also has nice temperatures and the riot of autumn colors. With the area's humidity, both summer and winter can be hell, with summer sweltering and winter biting cold. The good weather had apparently melted away the tendency to misbehave, because we'd had no cases come in over the transom since mid-July, and even Quincy's law firm hadn't sent us a case to work. Not that I mind taking their money for doing nothing, it's just that I don't like sitting around doing nothing. That's the way my folks taught me, a day's work for a day's pay. The not liking being bored part is all mine.

"So, you're bored, are you? Well, next case I get, I'll let you tag along as an observer. Ain't quite the same as actively investigating, but at least you won't have to be sitting in your office staring at the walls."

I'm not much of a passive bystander, but his offer *was* better than sitting in my office staring at the Potomac River and the Washington Ship Channel through the gaps in the trees surrounding the condos behind my office, or staring at my computer screen as the damn machine trounced me in yet another game of computer chess. Besides, Buster was working homicide now, so any case he got was likely to be interesting.

"Okay, you got yourself a deal," I said.

Just at that very moment, his phone buzzed. He took it out.

"Mayweather," he said, and then listened, nodding frequently. Finally, he said, "Okay, I'm rolling now. Tell the officer on scene I'll be bringing a civilian observer with me." He swiped the screen of his phone to turn it off and stuffed it back into his pocket. "How's that for service, eh. You got something to do."

"An interesting case?" I asked. It pretty much had to be, since he worked homicide. I just hoped it wasn't a gang shooting or something, because they often left collateral damage in the form of innocent bystanders. I've seen a lot of dead bodies in my time, but kids still get to me.

"Just might be. We'll know when we get there," he said. "Drink your tea, and let's roll. I'm parked around the corner, so follow me."

I'd lucked out and found a spot almost directly in front of Mom's plate glass window to park my bright green classic VW, which I affectionately call 'The Bug,' and for a change had actually arrived ahead of Buster.

"Okay, lunch is on me," I said, draining my tea in one long gulp and heading for the counter where Mom, in all her 300-pound glory, wrapped in a lime-green one-piece made of enough material to make a four-man tent, waited near the register.

She smiled as I approached, holding out my credit card. Normally, she'd make a fuss if you didn't eat all your food, and I'd left nearly half of mine on the plate, but she obviously had seen Buster on the phone, and knew the drill, so she just smiled and took my card.

"You enjoy yo lunch, hon?" she asked in that girlish voice of hers. I've never been able to figure out how such a tiny, beautiful voice comes out of such a large person.

"It was great, as usual," I said. "Sorry we have to eat and run, though>"

"I know how it is," she said, as she rang up the charges and ran my card. "That's okay. Next time you two boys come in, I'm gon' have somethin' special fo you, okay?"

"I can hardly wait." And, that was totally true. Mom's food, prepared lovingly by her husband of a whole bunch of years, is probably putting Buster and me on the road to clogged arteries, but it brings back memories of my childhood, sitting in my grandmother's kitchen while she fried chicken, vegetables, and bread—people in the part of Texas where I grew up fry just about everything—and, it tastes like what heaven must be like.

I grabbed the receipt from her, stuffed card and receipt in my pocket, and dashed out the door just as

Buster came around the corner in his 2002 Electric Blue Buick Century. The engine growled, he'd had the factory V-6 swapped out for a V-8, as he tapped the gas pedal, and the damn thing seemed like it wanted to pounce on something. Despite the tricked-out engine, it was the most conservative looking car Buster had driven in a long time. In addition, it came of a Canadian assembly line, breaking his tradition of driving only American-made cars. "Besides," he'd said, when I kidded him about it. "Canada is almost like America."

I couldn't rag him too much. I mean, how many six-foot, two hundred-pound ex-Special Ops guys do you know who drive a VW Beetle, and a bright green one at that?

I was slipping behind the wheel when he drove past, and even at a crawling speed, the Century's power was apparent. It *was* a beast waiting to pounce.

And, I felt a bit the same.

Chapter 3

The house was located on L Street, between First Street Northwest and North Capitol Street, a few blocks west of the Trailways bus station and the railroad tracks leading from Union Station, not far enough, though that on a quiet day you couldn't hear the trains. The neighborhood wasn't run down, but it definitely wasn't upscale either. Soot-covered brick buildings with tiny yards, or concrete pads instead of grass, cracked sidewalks, and more potholes in the streets than street. There was just enough space between the houses to fit a large recycle bin, but only a few were in evidence. Overturned trash containers lay scattered about, some in the street, where they'd been tossed by the trash truck workers after they'd been emptied.

There was nothing remarkable about the place. In fact, if not for the four white, red, and blue DC Metro cop cars with the flashing blue lights, the coroner's van, and the crime scene investigation unit van, you might have driven by it without even noticing. At 2:00 in the afternoon, with uniformed and plainclothes men and women going in and out, and sniffing around the perimeter of the place, it was the most noticeable house on the block. Neighbors stood on their front pads or hung out of their windows watching the action. A group of eight young men, two black, one white and five swarthy Hispanic, with their pants hanging just below their skinny buttocks, stood across the street, pointing and laughing. On any other day, the cops might have rousted them and made them move along, but homicide trumps everything, so they were ignored.

Buster drove past and parked a block beyond, blocking a fire hydrant to give me room to pull in behind. I gave my doors an extra check to make sure they were locked, and looked inside to make sure nothing was visible on the seats or dash that might invite someone to break in. I noticed that even though Buster had the POLICE – ON DUTY sign to put on his dash, he did the same thing. Sad as it is, in the 'hood, any unguarded valuable, regardless of who it belongs to, is fair game.

We walked back to the scene. The yellow crime scene tape had been strung up around the entire house, using two garbage containers on the sidewalk and the recycle containers on either side. I wondered if the neighbor who owned the containers being used had objected, and then decided, probably not. New York might be *the* city where people mind their own business, but Washington, DC has to be running a close second.

As we approached the tape, a uniformed cop, a young white guy who didn't look old enough yet to shave, held up a hand. Buster flashed his shield and pointed at me, "He's with me," he growled. The young cop saluted and lifted the tape for us.

I noticed as we walked toward the concrete pad that served as a front porch that the yard was mostly bare patches of earth with a few sickly-looking clumps of yellowing grass struggling to survive. The pad was, unlike the neighbor's place where a small wicker chair and matching table sat, as bare as the lawn.

The room we entered, which could be called a living room only because it had a sofa and coffee table against one wall, didn't really look lived in. There was a coating of dust on the coffee table, and no indication that anything had disturbed it for quite some time. A uniformed officer was walking along the wall opposite the sofa, looking for who knows what, while a jumpsuit-clad CSI technician was dusting the window sill for prints. Opposite the front door was an open way that from what I could see led into the kitchen, and next to that an open door with a downward-sloping ceiling which undoubtedly led to the basement.

A female officer, about five-four, with an attractive medium brown face under her uniform cap, but from the shoulders down looked like she'd been constructed from concrete blocks, stood near the door. She smiled when she saw Buster. "Hey, lieutenant, they tag you for this one?"

"Hey, Esther," Buster said. "Yeah, they must've known I was right in the middle of lunch. Hey, Al, this here's Patrol Officer Esther Jackson, toughest beat cop in Northwest, or anywhere else for that matter. Esther, meet my friend, Al Pennyback."

She stuck out a hand that was as large as mine.

"I heard 'bout you," she said. "You one bad ass private detective. Big, too."

She smiled up at me. If I wasn't already spoken for, and if she'd been about six inches taller, I might've been interested. Not today, though.

"Not all that bad," I said. "Not nearly as bad as Buster here."

"Yeah, he bad ass, too." She smiled again briefly, and then put on her cop face. "Sergeant Lopez already down there waitin' for you, loo. It's a bad one, a real, really bad one down there."

"Thanks, Esther. You keep things tight up here."

"You know it," she said, shooting me another hundred-watt smile as I squeezed past her and started down the stairs in Buster's wake.

It was noisier in the basement, and more crowded, too. But, it was the smell that really caught my attention. It hit about halfway down the stairs, like a sharp left jab from a top-ranked heavyweight.

First, there was that combination of dust, mold, and mildew that basements get when they're not aired out frequently, but it was the odor hanging over that that really got to me. The coppery smell I remembered so well from my combat days, blood exposed to air, along with the smell of sweat, feces, and urine, and the slightly sweet odor of flesh that has just begun to decay. I took a handkerchief from my pocket and placed it over my nose, not that it did much good. The contents of my stomach roiled, but I was able to choke it back. Buster had also put a handkerchief over his nose.

At the bottom of the stairs, a beanpole of a man, wearing a natty three-piece brown suit, with slicked back hair and a haughty look on his face, waited for us. He waved up at us, smiling wanly. Detective Sergeant Manuel 'Manny' Lopez, a sixteen-year veteran of the force, had been Buster's partner for eight months, since Buster was assigned to homicide. I'd never worked with him, but had met him a time or two at Buster's house, and he struck me as a competent cop and a nice guy.

As we reached the bottom of the stairs and stepped onto the rough concrete floor of the basement, from where I had to look up at Lopez's six-four height, he took a jar from his jacket pocket and passed it to Buster.

"Hey, partner, hey, Al," he said. "This is Mentholatum, rub it under your nose. It might sting a little, but It'll help cut down the smell."

Buster opened the jar and dipped his index finger in. He scooped out a bead of the milky ointment and rubbed it into his mustache. The stuff had a strong smell, that I picked up on as soon as he opened the jar. He passed it to me, and I copied his action, feeling a slight sting on my upper lip, and a cool flow of air up my nostrils. The stuff was *strong*, not quite erasing the smell of death, but making it manageable.

In addition to Lopez, there was another uniformed officer standing near the foot of the stairs, looking like it was all he could do to keep from hurling his lunch over the floor, a photographer snapping rapid-fire shots with a large digital SLR camera, a tech dusting for fingerprints, one scanning the room for trace evidence, and two emergency medical technicians bending over a big, queen-sized iron frame bed against the far wall. Beyond them, atop a wrinkled and dirty mattress, I could see to gnarled, bare feet, toes pointing toward the ceiling. The feet were attached to wrinkled lower legs. From the size and condition, I guessed an elderly man.

"Whatcha got here, Manny?" Al asked

"White male, mid- to late-seventies. His throat's been cut, and he has another puncture wound in his chest. According to the record of house ownership, he's likely Gabriel Birdsong, but we won't know for sure until the ME confirms identity with next of kin, assuming we can find one. The ME will have to say for sure, but the decomp I see, looks like the body's been here for a few days."

Buster walked toward the two EMTs, bumping against a plain, wooden chair that sat centered on the bed, about four feet away. At the sound of the chair scrapping across the concrete, the two techs turned. One, I could now see, was a woman, with a pixie face and light brown hair cut short. Her partner, about the same size, was a young, man with skin the color of café latte, and tightly curled black hair. I'd never seen either before, but from their expressions, they knew Buster.

"Lieutenant Mayweather," the woman said. "When can we move the body?"

"Lemme take a look first," he said.

Buster pushed between them. I walked toward the foot of the bed to get a clearer look, and immediately wished I hadn't.

I've seen violent death, seen it many times, and I've never gotten used to it. The dead no longer look human for some reason, and when the death was violent, that lack of a link to humanity is even less apparent.

I'd guessed right. What was left on the ratty sheet had been an elderly white man. He lay there, nude and on his back, his legs splayed out. The wrinkled calves were joined to flabby thighs by knobby, scabby knees. His tiny, flaccid penis stuck up in the air, looked like a shriveled brown mushroom resting on two large brown prunes. Above his thighs, a flabby belly flared out to the sides, with folds of love handles at the waist. In the center of his chest was a slit, a fraction of an inch wide and two inches long with dark droplets of drying and dried blood around the edges. The ragged edges of skin around the slit were gray. It was when I got to his neck, though, that my bile threatened to rise. On the left side of a wrinkled, grey neck, was a slash that started just under his left ear lobe, and ran down diagonally across his neck and sliced across his Adam's apple. It gaped open like some obscene, toothless mouth. The grey skin of his neck was covered with black, sticky blood which was crusty around the edges. A pattern of reddish black decorated the wall beside the bed like some garish abstract painting. The pillow and the sheet under his head and shoulders was black and sticky looking in a pattern that draped over the edge of the bed and down to the floor.

The lack of blood around and below the chest wound told me that his throat had been cut first, and his heart had already stopped pumping before he was stabbed there. Talk about overkill.

Lopez moved up beside me.

"Somebody really had it in for this old dude," he said.

"I don't know," I said. "It looks almost like some kind of ritual killing to me."

He rubbed at his smooth chin, reminding me that I needed a shave.

"What makes you say that?" Buster asked. He had to be as affected by the sight as I was, but Buster was all professional now, keeping a placid expression on his dark brown face and a calm tone in his voice.

"To start with, he's naked," I said. "Then, the throat looks like it was cut by someone who's done it before. No signs of hesitation, just one quick slash that had to sever his carotid and surely cut through his larynx. He would've probably bled out in a few seconds from a cut like that. The stab wound to the chest seems to have been . . . I don't know, part of some ceremony."

Lopez grunted. "Shit, that's all we need, some kinda devil cult operatin' in the neighborhood."

"Let's not make assumptions," Buster snapped. He looked around, getting everyone's attention. I knew he was as serious as a train wreck. Whenever Buster drops the street patios, and speaks like the Rhodes' Scholar he almost was, you'd better listen. "We don't know what the hell happened here, and until we do, no speculations, especially not about things like cults. No sense causing panic in the neighborhood. Manny, get the uniforms out canvassing the neighborhood. See if anyone saw or heard anything. You techs about finished in here yet?"

The slightly built Asian looking for trace evidence, the pockets of his jumpsuit stuffed with plastic evidence bags, and a box of already filled bags at his knee, looked up. I recognized him; Tommy Nguyen, a Vietnamese-American who had been recruited right out of college, and a whiz at spotting tiny bits of evidence. "Almost, boss," he said. "Just got to do the far corner."

"What about the body," Buster asked. "Can it be moved?"

The photographer, a slightly overweight, brown-skinned man with a modified, out-of-date afro, who I also recognized as Hector Lewis, held up his camera. "Yeah, they can bag him," he said. "I have all the shots of him I need. I'd like to get some shots of the bed with the body moved anyway."

Buster waved at the two EMTs. "Okay, bag him and tag him."

It wasn't as hard as it could've been. The body had been there long enough for the stiffness of rigor mortis to have faded. They had him inside a black, plastic body bag and on their gurney in seconds, and were soon maneuvering the gurney and its grisly load up the narrow stairs. When they were gone, Buster pulled me aside.

"You sure about that ritualistic killin' shit, bro?" he asked quietly.

"No, I'm not. It has some of the signs, but on the other hand, if it had been some kind of ritual, I'd think there'd be other evidence, like candlewax or something. Whoever did it, though, really wanted this old man dead."

"Shit, I hope the hell you're wrong. Ever since the DC sniper case last year, just saying ritual, serial, or spree killing around the precinct has the suits running for the antacid. We don't need a repeat of that."

I fully understood his concern. From October 3, 2002 until their arrest on October 24 when they were found sleeping in their car, 42-year-old John Allen Muhammed and his 17-year-old accomplice, Lee Boyd Malvo, had terrorized the DC area, shooting from ambush, killing ten people and wounding three others in Maryland, DC, and Virginia. For 21 days, the entire area was tense, with people afraid to stop at gas stations or mow their lawns. After the two were captured, it was discovered that they'd been involved in a spree of killing and robbery from the state of Washington to Georgia. He was right, the area couldn't stand another episode like that.

"You're right," I said. "Until we know more, it's homicide by person or persons unknown. Maybe when you dig into the victim's background, you'll find there's some personal connection."

He nodded. "Now, that I can handle."

Jackson, walking sideways to negotiate the narrow stairwell, came halfway down.

"Lieutenant Mayweather," she called. "There's someone up here wants to talk to you."

"If it's a reporter, tell them to call headquarters and talk to our PR guy."

"It's not a reporter. It's a lady says she sister of the man who owns the house."

"Okay, tell her I'll be right up." He turned to the techs. "I want a full report of everything you find here, no matter how small or insignificant."

They nodded, and he headed for the stairs. Thankfully, I followed. Even with the body gone, the smell of blood and body waste, the odor of death, still hung heavily in the air, despite the Mentholatum.

Chapter 4

Even with the dustiness and odor from not having been cleaned in a while, the air in the living room was like a fresh spring breeze compared to the basement. I took a deep breath as soon as I was a few feet away from the basement door. Jackson, standing across the room near the open door to the outside, laughed.

"I know how you feel. You can still smell it where you standing, but it ain't as bad as bein' down there in it, so you probably don't notice."

Buster kept walking across the room until he stood beside her. He took a deep breath.

"She's right," he said. "Smells a hell of a lot better here."

She turned up her nose. "But, you don't, loo. That smell done got in your clothes."

He sniffed at his shoulder and made a face. "Damn, you're right. I just bought this suit three months ago, now I'm gon' have to throw it in the trash."

I sniffed at my sleeve. Jackson was right. The smell from the basement was in my clothing. I didn't have Buster's problem. I was wearing an old pair of khaki pants and a slightly less old plaid shirt, so junking them wouldn't present any problem. Getting home before Sandra to do it before she got a whiff, on the other hand, would try some tricky maneuvering.

"The lady who wanted to see you is outside," Jackson said. "She came in, but took one sniff and decided she'd rather wait out there. Oh yeah, she got here just as they were taking the vic out. They let her take a look. She IDed him as her brother, Gabriel Birdsong. Pretty near freaked out when she saw what'd been done to his throat."

"Is she calmed down now?"

"Yeah, Sergeant Lopez is out there with her. He pretty good at stuff like that. Calmed her right down."

"Okay, thanks," Buster said. "Have the uniforms turned up anything yet?"

"Nope, you know how it is, lieutenant, nobody saw nothing, nobody heard nothing, nobody knows nothing."

The police are supposed to protect and serve, and the DC cops do a fairly good job of it, better than many of the forces throughout the country, but it doesn't keep people in the poor neighborhoods, regardless of their color or ethnicity, from being leery of them. It can also be hazardous to your health to be seen talking to the fuzz, on the off chance that the crime being investigated was committed by one or other of the drug gangs in the District. The drug dealers don't like snitches, and witnesses are just another variety of snitch to them. The life expectancy of a snitch in some of these neighborhoods is only marginally longer than a pedophile's in prison, if they're lucky. Survival trumps civic-mindedness.

Buster shook his head in frustration. As much as I would like to have said something encouraging at that moment, I knew to keep my mouth shut. Hell, there was nothing encouraging to say. He turned and walked out onto the concrete porch, and I followed.

Lopez stood just off the porch, on the cracked and uneven walk that led out to the even more cracked and uneven sidewalk. He had a solicitous look on his movie-star handsome face and was holding a handkerchief out to a short, skinny, pale woman wearing a brown coat, despite the lack of chill in the air, over a lighter brown dress that was three inches longer and stopped mid-calf on skinny legs encased in off-white hose. She wore what Sandra calls sensible shoes, the kind with widely-rounded toes and low heels. Her narrow, pale face, with a straight nose that turned down a tad at the tip, with the grey-streaked brown hair pulled severely back into a neat bun at the back of her head gave her the look of a no-nonsense nanny from a British period TV show, or, if she'd been wearing black, with one of those conical hats and a cape, like the witch in *The Wizard of Oz*. Even wearing brown, she looked faded, like a character from a black and white TV show, or one of those sepia-toned photographs. Her cheeks were streaked with tears and her rounded shoulders heaved. Lopez patted her on the shoulder.

"I am so sorry for your loss, Ms. Abel," he was saying. "Here, would you like my handkerchief to wipe your face?"

She mumbled something and took the proffered cloth and dabbed at her cheeks, only succeeding in smearing the powder that hadn't added any color to her face.

Lopez turned at the sound of our footsteps on the concrete pad.

"Hey, Bus-, er, Lieutenant Mayweather," he said. "This is Ms. Constance Abel, she's the sister of the victim."

Buster stuck out a hand. "Ms. Abel," he said. "I'm so sorry for your loss, but rest assured, we're gonna find who did this."

"T-thank you," she said as she grasped his hand, her's immediately lost in the fold of his giant mitt. "What happened? Who would d-do such a ghastly thing?"

"We don't know yet, ma'am. I know this is hard on you, but do you mind if I ask a few questions?"

She looked uncertain. Her watery brown eyes roamed over Buster's face. He looked back with a sympathetic expression. She bobbed her head up and down.

"Of course, anything if it'll help find out who did this."

"Did your brother, Mr. Birdsong, have any enemies? Anyone who would want to do him harm?

She hesitated before answering. I would've put it down to the circumstances, after all, she'd just seen her brother in a body bag with his throat gaped open, but there was something in the way her eyes darted to the side just before she spoke that triggered alarm bells in my brain.

"Uh, no," she said. "Gabe didn't get out much. I don't think he knew that many people."

"Did he live here alone?"

I noticed the eye flicker again. She looked nervous.

"No, my niece, Lena, our niece, that is, was his caretaker."

Buster's eyebrows did a little wiggle, an almost imperceptible movement that most people wouldn't have noticed. But, I'm not most people. I notice things, things like the fact that Constance Abel was not telling us everything she knew. I noticed that Buster's interest had been aroused by the knowledge that there was a possibility that another person who could be identified had been in the house with the victim.

"How old is your niece?" he asked.

"Well, let me think." She scrunched her eyes shut, then snapped them open. "Yes, she would've been 19 last month."

Buster took a pad from his jacket, flipped it open and began writing.

"What's your niece's full name?"

"Lena Marie Birdsong. Her father was our younger brother Bartholomew. He and his wife were killed in a car accident when Lena was eleven. Gabe and I were her only living relatives, but my husband, rest his soul, wasn't comfortable taking in a pre-teen, so she came to live with Gabriel."

Buster made some more notes. "Ms. Abel, do you know where your niece is now?" he asked.

"No, she should've been here. Ever since she graduated from high school last year, she pretty much stays close to home, except for the occasional trip to the store. My brother wasn't exactly very mobile, and taking care of him stifled Lena's social life a bit, I'm afraid."

Her brow was wrinkled and her eyes kept darting from side to side, but always coming back to the front door, as if she expected someone to come walking through it. She was worried about something.

"There was no one else here when we arrived," Buster said. He pointed at Lopez. "Grab a couple of the techs and a uniform and search the house from top to bottom." Lopez nodded and hurried off. "Do you know where your niece might go? Does she have a car?"

"No, she doesn't even have a driver's license. She and Gabriel either walked or took the bus everywhere. I don't think the poor child's ever even been on the subway."

I don't know what was going through Buster's mind, but mine was awash with possibilities. Now, in addition to a mutilated, naked stiff, we had a missing girl, well, woman actually. I don't know why I thought 'we,' since this was a police matter, and I had no client, but something about it intrigued me. Truth be known, everything about it was beginning to intrigue me. That's the problem when you're an action type who can't resist an unsolved puzzle and your main job's not providing you with enough stimulation. You stand around fantasizing.

Buster's voice broke me out of my reverie. "We'll be on the lookout for your niece, ma'am," he said. "And, if you think of anything, anything at all that might help us determine who did this, I want you to give me a call." He handed her one of his cards. "In the meantime, would you like for one of our officers to drive you home?"

She looked like she'd been off in some dreamland. She blinked and shook herself. "Uh, no, I'll walk to the

Metro, the New York Avenue Station's not that far from here."

"Okay." He turned to me. "Sorry to dump you, pal," he said. "But, this case just got a whole lot more complicated. Now, in addition to looking for a murder suspect, I have a possible . . . missing person." Or a prime suspect, I know he wanted to say, but had held back because that suspect's aunt was standing there.

He was right about the case being complicated, but it was also weird. I don't know what his teams would find on the second floor, but the brief walk-through I'd had of the living room hadn't shown any signs of someone else living in the house, least of all a girl just out of her teens. And, there was that bed in the basement—what was with that?

"No problem, amigo," I said. "I was planning to knock of early and take Sandra out for dinner anyway."

He flashed me a smile and turned to reenter the house. I stood there, wondering how I was going to insert myself into this case.

Charles Ray

Chapter 5

Constance Abel solved my problem.

"I recognize you," she said. "You're that private investigator the *Post* is always writing about, aren't you?"

Guilty as charged, although *always* is a bit of an exaggeration. My friend Lucia Garcia Mendez, a feature writer for the *Washington Post*, writes the occasional human-interest piece about me—about once every four months or so—when it's an otherwise slow news week. Lucy's been a chronicler of my career for over a decade, ever since we met when I was investigating the drive-by shooting of a student in one of Sandra's classes at Carter High, the inner-city school where she teaches. Lucy dubbed me 'The Brown Knight' early on, and the damned moniker stuck. Thanks to the occasional photo she ran with her articles, in some circles I was well-known, a local celebrity of sorts.

"Uh, yes," I said. "I am a private investigator." I'm also modest to a fault.

"Well, I think I might have need of your services."

That was a question I wasn't expecting.

"I'm sorry, ma'am, but I don't do murder investigations. I leave that to the police."

She looked at me as if I'd just opened my fly and pissed on her shoes.

"I'm not asking you to investigate a murder," she said, in a tone of voice a teacher would use on a student who'd just recited the alphabet after being asked to solve an algebra problem.

"Then, why do you need me?"

"Look. I might be old, but I'm not stupid. I saw the look in that cop's face when I mentioned Lena." She stamped her foot. "She's missing, and my brother's dead, and he thinks maybe she did it and ran away."

She was right on all counts. She *did* look old, older even than the corpse they'd just carted away. And, I was pretty sure that Buster did consider the missing girl a prime suspect. After all, most murder victims know their killer, and more times than people might care to admit, that killer is a family member. I could understand his reasoning. I didn't necessarily always agree with it, because when you took that point of view, there was always the danger it would blind you to the truth. I had to defend my friend, though.

"I'm sure that's not the case, ma'am," I said. "Lieutenant Mayweather is just being thorough and careful. You still haven't said why you need my services, though."

"That should be obvious. If Lena was here, they would've found her by now, so that means she's missing. That means someone took her, probably the same person who killed my brother."

"I'm not sure I can buy that scenario," I said. "If she was here, and possibly witnessed the murder, why didn't the killer just—"

"How would I know that," she interrupted me, making a chopping motion with her gnarled hand. "That's what I want to hire you to find out. I want you to find my niece."

"But, Ms. Abel, the police are better equipped to do that. Besides, my services don't come cheap." Which, is actually not true. For those in need who lack the resources to pay, Heather and I charge less, and on occasion even take their cases pro bono. I don't usually advertise that up front, though.

"I'm not a rich woman, Mr. Pennyback, but I'm also not without resources. What are your fees?"

"A thousand bucks a day, plus expenses, and we usually ask for a thousand-dollar retainer to get started."

She didn't even blink. "Do you take checks?"

"Uh, yes," I said.

She reached into the oversized purse she had hung on her arm, and pulled out a black leatherette folder. Waving for me to turn around, she used my back as a writing desk. I could feel her sweeping motions as she filled out a check. She had firm, sure strokes. While she looked to be in her eighties, probably south of the middle-eighties, she still had a lot of fire in her. When she'd finished, she tapped my shoulder.

"You can turn around now."

When I did, she handed me a check on a well-known local bank, made out to Al Pennyback in the amount of one thousand dollars. Her expression, worried before, was now steelier, like she'd just achieved some goal of which I was unaware.

I usually consult with Heather before accepting cases, trusting her judgment more than my own, but this case had piqued my curiosity, and I was pretty sure she'd go along with it. She has a soft spot for stray animals, old people, and kids in trouble, and this had two of the three. I took the check, folded it neatly and slipped it into my shirt pocket. I then took out one of my cards and handed it to her.

"I'll need you to come to my office and sign a contract," I said. "Do you have any problems getting to the waterfront area?"

"None whatsoever. How far are you from the metro station there?"

"Just a few blocks." I often used the metro system to get around town, to avoid the hassle of finding parking or dealing with DC-area traffic. This time of year, the walk from the Waterfront Metro to my office would actually be quite nice.

"That's not a problem," she said. "I use the metro a lot, and don't mind walking. What time should I come to your office?"

I looked at my watch. It was getting late, and I was anxious to get home.

"Anytime on Monday would be fine. I'll let my partner, Heather Bunche know to expect you."

"Good. I'll see you Monday."

"Oh, and one other thing. When you come, please bring anything that will help us in finding your niece, like recent photographs.

"Of course," she said. Then, she spun on her heels, and with a sprightly step for someone of her age, set off northeast, in the direction of the New York Avenue Metro station.

Well, I now had a legitimate excuse to pry into the case. I was mulling an investigative strategy over in my mind, when Buster came out of the house. He had a strange look on his face.

"Find anything useful?" I asked.

"Nada. The techs found lots of trace evidence in the basement, but it'll take days to get it analyzed. No sign of a weapon, or at least, not a weapon that could've cut the old man's throat like that. Oh, and if there was a woman, or girl, living with the old man, she left no traces, not even women's clothing in the closets upstairs."

"No photos?"

"No, nothing," he said. "Except for men's clothing and shoes that are about the size to fit the deceased, there's no indication of any other inhabitant."

"The aunt was pretty definite about the niece living here," I said. "Said she's been living with the old man since her folks died."

"I know. I was standing there when she said it. Maybe she moved out, and the aunt wasn't told."

"Maybe, maybe not. This is one strange case. But, the old woman's pretty sure of herself. She even hired me to find the niece."

Except for a slight twitch of his brows, he didn't react to that bit of news. Most cops resent having PIs sniffing around active cases, but Buster and I go way back. I've helped him close more than one case, and on occasion, he's even helped me on mine. He smiled.

"That might not be such a bad thing, bro," he said. "You're pretty good with the strange shit. Maybe while you're looking for this mythical niece, you'll see something we missed. Just keep me posted, okay?"

"Don't I always?"

He snorted at me. "No, and you know damn well you don't."

I held up my right hand in the three-finger Boy Scout oath sign. "I promise that, in this case, I will keep you informed of everything I learn."

And, at the time, I really meant it.

Chapter 6

Before leaving the scene, I called Heather, catching her at her desk, which was no surprise, and filled her in. She agreed that the case sounded interesting, so I gave her the details needed to draw up a contract, and told her to expect a call or visit from Constance Abel the following Monday. She assured me that she'd have it done before leaving for the day, and wished Sandra and me a good weekend. I then put my phone away, walked to my Volkswagen, and headed home.

With the late afternoon traffic, and having to cut across some of the city's busiest rush-hour arteries to get to River Road in Montgomery County, Maryland, I didn't get home until 6:30. Sandra had beaten me home by forty-five minutes.

I found her in the kitchen chopping lettuce and tomatoes, having surmised that I might be tied up and have to cancel our Friday evening out. When I got close, and she got a whiff of my clothing, she made a face that caused me to take a step backwards. In response to the stricken look on her face, I gave her the twenty-five-word or less version of the afternoon's events, and she turned to resume chopping.

"Hey, babe," I said. "This is our night to eat out."

"After the day you've had, I should think you'd want to stay home," she said.

I assured her that I had no such desire or intention, helped her put the veggies in plastic bags and store them in the fridge's crisper, with the promise that I'd make something special for Saturday lunch. Then, after dumping my smelly clothes on the back porch, showering for twenty minutes, and changing into fresh duds, we drove in her blue Prius because the Bug still had a residual odor of death in it, to a Vietnamese Pho restaurant on Rockville Pike.

Pho Hoa, was a recently-opened restaurant specializing in the traditional Vietnamese noodle soup, a tangy broth with thin slices of meat or chunks of seafood, basil, mint, lime, bean sprouts, and thick rice noodles, to which diners added a brown sauce, red pepper paste, and a drop or two of the pungent *nuoc man,* or fish sauce, which smelled terrible, but added a unique taste. I'd been introduced to *pho* during my brief time in Vietnam just as the war was ending and my unit was waiting for word of our redeployment to the states. Little old ladies had set up little stands just outside our base camp near Pleiku, from which they sold lukewarm *33,* the local Vietnamese beer, warm Coca-Cola, and *pho,* which was served in bent tin bowls or beat up mess kits they'd salvaged from the nearby dump. I remembered it fondly, partly because I'd discovered it just when I was getting ready to put the war behind me, and partly because I was fascinated watching the thin slices of meat cook in the hot broth before my eyes. Oh, and it tasted great, and was a great hangover tonic after a night of drinking too many beers.

The shopping center was one of many that line both sides of Rockville Pike, a collection of one-story dark grey buildings arranged in a blocky U shape with the base at the back of the lot and parking in the middle. Except for the small signs over the front entrances, all of the buildings looked the same, but inside *Pho Hoa* they entered a different world.

Bare tables, each with four chairs, were arranged in three rows in the long, narrow space, one row against each wall, and one down the center. In the back was a high counter behind which sat a demure looking Vietnamese lady who presided over the work of the three Hispanic busboys and two Vietnamese waitresses dressed in white blouses with the top three buttons undone exposing the cleavage between their small breasts and black miniskirts that ended mid-thigh. I noticed signs for domestic and imported beer on the wall at the entrance, under the large hand-printed menu listing the twelve different kinds of *pho*, and understood. The sign at the door gave the operating hours as Noon to Midnight, meaning that after the usual supper hour, it was a hangout for local Asian men, Vietnamese, Chinese, and Korean, to drink and socialize, which explained the provocative attire on the waitresses.

Now, though, it was occupied by the dinner crowd. Two Vietnamese families were at the tables on the wall at the entrance, the parents looking frustrated while the kids, preteens all, looked like your typical rambunctious American brats, loud voices, louder clothes and all. Against the far wall, a mixed black-white group of men and women dressed in business attire, had pulled two tables together and were talking with in hushed tones with a lot of waving of their hands as they used chopsticks and plastic spoons to shovel the soup into their mouths. There were a few couples scattered about, mostly Asian, and three Hispanic laborers eating spring rolls. One of the waitresses rushed over to us. In heavily accented English, she welcomed us and suggested a table near the back. It had a buffer of two empty tables, so we wouldn't have to put up with listening to our neighbors' conversations unless the place got more crowded, and it was closer to the kitchen, so we could see our food being prepared. Unlike a lot of people, I actually like being near the kitchen when I dine out. Maybe it's just my suspicious neighbor, but I like to see what people are doing when they're messing with my food.

After we were seated, the waitress took our order. We both decided against beer, opting instead for glasses of ice water. I usually ordered a big bowl of noodle soup when I ate lunch, which was quite filling, but since this was a night out, we asked for small bowls of their *pho dac biet*, the special *pho* that contained eye round, flank steak, tripe, and meat balls; *banh cam*, deep-fried glutinous rice and sesame balls filled with sweet mung bean paste; and *cha gio*, fried spring rolls made of pork wrapped in thin rice paper.

She brought our water right away, and while we waited for the cook, an elderly Vietnamese man wearing a chef's hat and sleeveless tee shirt, prepared our food.

After taking a sip of water, Sandra held her glass in front of her face and gave me a pensive look.

"That crime scene must have really hit you hard," she said. "You look kind of sad."

"I always am when I see violent death," I said. "I didn't know that old guy, but as John Donne said, 'every man's death diminishes me.' It all seems so senseless."

"Murder is a senseless crime, babe, and murderers are senseless and unfeeling people. At least you got a case out of it, and I know how important that is to you."

I lifted my water glass in a toast. "You know me all too well, my dear."

Hell, it didn't take a Sherlock Holmes to know that I was itching for something to do. I'd been moping around the house for weeks, never really saying anything, but she'd lived with me long enough to know it was because I was like an old fire horse, kept in the stable too long. I was itching for something to catch fire so I could get back into action.

"So, what are you going to do to find the missing niece?"

Leave it to my Sandra to cut to the chase; no beating about the bush, or asking meaningless questions. She gets right to the heart of the matter.

"I'll have to start with some research into Lena Birdsong and her family," I said. "I'm hoping Heather's already started a basic background check. Heck, I don't even have the faintest idea what she looks like, there were no pictures in the old man's house, and the cops didn't find any women's clothes when they searched."

She wrinkled her nose. "That's strange."

"Just one of the many strange things about this case."

"Strange is good, right." She smiled at me. "I know you. The tougher the puzzle, the more you like it."

Ordinarily, she'd be right, but something smelled like three-day-old fish about this case. I just couldn't put my finger on what it was.

"Except, a girl's life could be at stake," I said.

She frowned. "Yes, that does up the ante quite a bit. But, I have complete faith in you. If anyone can find her, it's you and Heather."

"Yeah, unless she's an alien sent here to live secretly among us, there's a record of her somewhere, and Heather will find it."

And, that's no empty brag. Heather can coax information from computer files that their originators think they have protected. I make it a point not to ask her how she does it, just in case I'm ever called to testify in her hacking case, I can honestly say I knew nothing about it. Of course, the main reason I never ask—anymore—is that the one time I did ask, I didn't understand a single thing she said. I heard words like firewalls and trojan horses and backdoors, and she might as well have been speaking Martian.

"You know," Sandra said. "The name Birdsong is not that common, and when you mentioned it just now, it triggered a memory. I've run across it somewhere, I just have to remember where."

"That would be helpful if you could." I reached over and took hold of her wrist. Her skin was soft and warm, and I could feel the racing of her pulse under my fingers. "But, I have something else I need you to do first."

She raised her eyes without lifting her head. Man, was that sexy. It hit me right in the—you can guess where. She smiled, and I got a double jolt, this time a warm feeling of a non-painful punch to the heart.

I signaled for the waitress to bring the bill.

Charles Ray

Chapter 7

The harder she tried to remember, the more the pain throbbed behind her eyes. She'd given up trying to get out of her bonds; the duct tape had been wound around her wrists many, many times, and tight to the point of almost cutting off circulation, and the old-fashioned iron manacles around her ankles, attached to a shiny steel chain that was bolted to the wall that she leaned against, resisted her effort to loosen them.

After an hour of useless struggling against her restraints, she'd given up, lay back against the wall and cried for another hour. After she had no more tears, she became angry.

Why am I here? Something was wrong. There was something she was supposed to remember, but she couldn't form the images in her mind.

What did I do wrong? She wondered why she thought that, then another thought occurred. *Of course, I did something wrong. It's because I'm a bad girl. But, why am I a bad girl? What did I do that was so bad?*

Someone brought her here. Had to be. She certainly didn't wrap her own wrists with duct tape, and she was pretty sure she'd never owned ankle manacles of the type that were clamped tightly around her ankles.

She felt a tickling sensation in her loins, and realized that she had to pee. She looked around wildly, taking deep breaths almost to the point of hyperventilating. When she was finally able to slow her breathing, she saw the large ten-gallon bucket a few feet away to her right. She couldn't move more than a few feet forward, but she found that by scooting on her butt, she was able to reach the bucket. She looked in. It was empty.

The thought of what she would have to do made her stomach roil. *In a bucket for fuck sake. That's uncivilized. Ugh.* Then, she thought of the alternative. *Double-ugh. And, it would start to itch like hell later.* So, even though it was clumsy, with her wrists taped together in front, she managed to get her jeans and panties down to her ankles and hoisted herself up until she was balanced on the tops of the back of her thighs. She felt almost orgasmic as her bladder emptied, then, there was another explosion of good feeling as her bowl emptied itself as well.

Finished, she looked around. *Shit, I don't have anything to wipe myself with. Well, that was a great idea. Now I have to either sit here naked, or have mud smears on my jeans and underwear.* She shrugged and pulled her clothes up, shuddering at the thought. She could already feel an itchy sensation in the area of her buttocks and crotch.

The son of a bitch who brought me here is going to pay for this. She just wished that she knew who it was. *I'll kick his balls up around his ears. No one does this to*—then, she realized that she didn't remember her name.

Now, she had a new question, *who the hell am I?*

Charles Ray

Chapter 8

I got up early on Monday, rousted Sandra out of bed too, and we went for a morning run. After a thirty-minute workout on the heavy bag in the barn out back of the house, I did a short meditation while Sandra showered, and then showered and changed. We had a light breakfast. She went off to Carter High, the inner-city school where she teaches, and I drove to my office via Clara Barton Parkway and Canal Road.

I long ago gave up trying to beat Heather to the office. In addition to living just over the Potomac in Northern Virginia, and having a shorter commute, she just likes to get in early and get her tea brewed and her computer fired up.

"So, I wasn't surprised when I walked through the door of our office at 8:15 and found her hunched over her laptop, scribbling on a notepad with her right hand, while holding a cup of some fragrant tea in her left. She looked up as I entered, blowing a stray lock of her ash blonde hair from in front of her left eye.

"Hey, boss man," she said. "Get yourself a cup of coffee and pull up a chair, so I can give you a data dump on our new case."

Heather is not a coffee drinker herself, but she always makes me a pot from the stash of Jamaican that I keep in my desk drawer. She even bought one of those new four-cup brewers that she keeps on the credenza beside her desk, along with a couple of my favorite mugs, big, white ceramic monstrosities with chips in the handles. I filled the one with the slogan, 'Don't talk to me until I've had my coffee' on it, and after taking a long, satisfying sip, I straddled the visitor chair at the side of her desk, rested my elbows on the edge of the desk, with the mug under my nose, enjoying the woodsy aroma.

"Okay, brain cells firing, ears wide open," I said. "Fire away."

She turned to face me, holding her notebook up. I noticed that she held it closer to her face than usual, and wondered if her vision was weakening. She spends a lot of time staring at a computer screen, and that can't be good for your eyes. Wisely, though, I decided not to mention it.

She ran a finger over the notebook page. "Lena Marie Birdsong, born September 2, 1984 to Bartholomew Leonard Birdsong and Marie Swan Birdsong, nee Clark. The parents died in a one-car crash on September 2, 1995, on their way home from a party at the home of Lauren and Andrew Vanderbilt, just south of Baltimore. According to the police report, Bartholomew was driving, and lost control of the car near Bowie. It went off the road and crashed into a tree, killing both of them instantly. The autopsy showed the presence of cocaine in both of them, and a quantity of cocaine was found in the car." She flipped to the next page. "Young Lena was at home with her grandfather, Gabriel, at the time. He and his older sister, Constance, were the only living relatives, and the court placed her in his custody."

I mulled that information in my mind. It jived, to a degree, with what the old lady had told me.

"So, she's been living with her grandfather since she was eleven?"

She nodded. "As far as I can determine from the records I've been able to unearth." She played with the stray lock of hair that kept dropping over her eyes, a problem she's been having ever since she let it grow longer. "There is one thing odd about it, though. Most girls her age have a presence all over social media, Facebook, Instagram, and the like, but I've not been able to find anything about her, not a thing. And, she doesn't have a driver's license or mobile phone account, or at least, not under her name."

Now, that *was* unusual. I don't know a lot about teenagers of either gender, and what I know about social media you could put in your eye and it wouldn't irritate it at all, but I *did* know that a teen without a social media presence or a smart phone that they were constantly using to text incomprehensible messages to each other, was not the norm. That, taken together with the lack of any signs of her at the house where she had supposedly been living for the past eight years made this one hell of a puzzle. It was as if she didn't exist.

"Have you been able to find any photos of her?" I asked.

"Not a one." She shook her head, looking as puzzled as I felt.

"I hope her aunt has a current one," I said. "It'll be hard enough trying to locate someone who has no phone—and, I take it no credit card?" She nodded to indicate that I'd guessed right. "But, without knowing what she looks like, it'll be like trying to find a needle in a stack of needles."

She looked puzzled. "You mean a needle in a haystack, right?"

"No, at least that way, you could feel around until something stuck you. I mean, if I don't know what she looks like, she could be standing right in front of me, and I wouldn't know it."

"Oh." She said it like she understood what I was talking about, but the perplexed look in her eyes said she didn't, not really.

I'm sort of used to that. I tend to let fly with things sometimes that make perfect sense to me, but are Greek to those around me, and being a generation older than Heather means that it happens more often than not.

"Do you have anything on the grandfather or the aunt?" I asked.

"Not much, other than they're both old, he's dead, and he was the girl's legal guardian since she was eleven."

'I guess, him being so old and all, his income was from retirement or Social Security?"

"Actually, he once owned a factory that made plastic containers, but he sold it for quite a large amount when his health started to worsen, and was living off that, and his savings. He wasn't exactly rich, but he wasn't eating cat food either."

I've never understood that analogy. Anyone who has ever owned a pet and had to pay the inflated prices they charge for canned pet food knows that if you can't afford a can of Spam, you can't afford dog or cat food. But, I knew what she was saying. Despite living in a rundown neighborhood, Gabriel Birdsong wasn't on the dole. All the more reason to find it strange that a teenager living with him would be all but invisible.

"What about the sister, our client?"

"Not much," she said. "She's five years older than Gabriel. Married Joseph Abel when she was twenty-two and moved out of the family house. Her husband died five years ago, and she lives alone. The husband was an executive in a construction company, and apparently, when he died his savings and insurance left her comfortable—just."

"No red flags on any of them?"

"Not even a traffic ticket. Neither Gabriel nor Constance owns or owned a car, at least not recently. Gabriel's driver's license expired five years ago, and as far as I can tell, Constance has never had one."

This family was starting to have 'strange' written all over it. I just couldn't put a proper label on it, so when in doubt, I did what I always do, I punted it to Heather. "Well, keep digging. There has to be something out there somewhere that will help us track this girl down."

In her own way, Heather's as obsessed with puzzles and challenges as I am. The difference is, she's obsessed with information, computers and electronic storage She refuses to admit that an electronic or even paper information can be hidden from her. I think that if I hadn't hired her to work for me when I started the PI company after the death of my wife and son, she would've become one of those reclusive hackers, breaking into government information systems just to prove she could do it. I, on the other hand, like physical things, things I can wrap my hands around, and I like being outdoors, and dealing with living, breathing people. It occurred to me that I hadn't really gotten a good look at Birdsong's neighborhood, and that I might get people to talk to me where they wouldn't talk to the cops.

I reminded Heather to expect a visit from Constance Abel, and headed out the door.

Chapter 9

The neighborhood looked worse the second time than it did the first, even without cop cars and flashing lights all over the place, or maybe it was because there were no flashing lights. At least, the emergency lights had added a touch of color. Without them, the whole neighborhood was a dingy brown and grey, soot and mold smeared, with gaping dark holes where broken windows hadn't been repaired. Even the graffiti looked indifferent.

I parked a block from the Birdsong house. No use spooking people right off the bat by associating myself with the grisly murder that took place in their midst. Of course, as soon as I started asking questions, the cat would be out of the bag, but, that was a stream I'd wade when I came to it.

Now, I had to decide how to start my investigation. I could hit the closer houses first, since they'd be the ones most likely to know what went on in Birdsong's place, but there was always the chance that the farther neighbors might have noticed something, and would, being farther away, more likely to be willing to share it with a stranger. Of course, there was also the possibility that no one would tell me anything. It was a mental coin flip; heads, the farther houses, tails, the ones closer in. I imagined a coin flipping in the air, and closed my eyes. I saw a flash of a rugged, noble profile and a feather headdress—yeah, I mentally flipped a nickel. Heads won, so I would start on the far perimeter and work my way inward.

I walked to the end of the block, and stopped in front of probably the neatest house there. A red-brick, one-story house that didn't have broken bottles or used condoms on the sidewalk, and with two neat flower pots with some red flowers flanking the entrance. I could see flowery curtains inside the windows. My guess was this was an elderly couple. I walked up the walk to the concrete slab that served as a porch. There was a black rubber welcome mat with the word, 'WELCOME' in fancy white script. I rang the bell. After a few minutes, the door opened a few inches, and a bright blue eye, framed by shiny white hair, peeked at me through the crack.

"Yes? What do you want?" a creaky voice asked.

I took out my PI card and held it up in front of the eye. "Sorry to bother you, ma'am. My name is Al Pennyback. I'm a private investigator working on a missing person case, and I was wondering if I might have a few moments of your time."

"Who's missing?"

"Do you know Lena Birdsong?"

"Lena who? I don't know nobody named Birdsong." The crack started to close.

"She's the granddaughter of the man who was killed down the block last week," I said quickly.

The door stopped closing.

"Oh, was that his name. Old guy, kinda scrawny looking, 'ceptin' for his belly?"

I hadn't paid that much attention to what Birdsong's anatomy looked like, but that seemed close. "Yes, that's him," I said.

"He had a granddaughter?"

"That's what his sister, Constance, told me. The granddaughter is missing, and Constance, Constance Abel, has hired me to find her."

"Don't know nothin' 'bout no granddaughter." The door slammed shut, and I heard the rattle of a security chain.

Strike one.

I moved on to the next house. The yard wasn't quite as neat, and there were no flowers flanking the door, but someone had power-washed the walls, because they weren't soot-streaked like most of the other houses on the block. I pushed the doorbell button. After a few seconds, the door swung inward, and I found myself staring up at a man of indeterminate age, about six inches taller, and probably fifty pounds heavier than me. He had a head that looked as big and round as a dark-brown pumpkin, bald on top with a fringe of tightly-curled white hair around the periphery, making him look like a cross between Uncle Ben on the rice package and a black version of the Green Giant.

"Yeah, what do you want?" he asked in a voice that tried to be gentle, but set up vibrations in my ears.

I showed him my ID.

"I was hired by the sister of the man down the block who was killed. She wants me to find her niece, his granddaughter. I'm canvassing the neighborhood to see if anyone knows what might have happened to her." I spit it out fast, just in case he decided to slam the door in my face. He surprised me by stepping aside instead.

"Come on in," he said. "I was just about to have a cup of coffee. You want one?"

I didn't, but when you're a guest in someone's home, and they offer you something to drink, it's rude to refuse.

"Sure, that sounds good."

He led me into a neat, tastefully furnished living room, and pointed to an old, but clean leather sofa.

"Have a seat, I'll be right back."

While he was gone, I looked around. The room was not all what I would have expected from a man his size. On the coffee table, he had a neat arrangement of fashion and movie magazines, and next to them was a fragile-looking crystal vase containing two yellow roses. Upon closer inspection, I noted they weren't plastic as I'd first suspected, but real flowers.

He came back holding two medium sized china coffee cups. The aroma coming from was the woody, fresh-brewed smell of Colombian. I know this because I have a good stock of Colombian beans at home. He placed one of the cups on the coffee table in front of me and sat on the other end of the sofa and began taking sips from his. I picked my cup up and held it under my nose, letting the aroma caress my smell sensors. I took a sip. It was strong, but not too strong. Just the way I like mine.

I put the cup down. "Thanks for taking the time to talk to me, Mister—"

"Carlton Jacobs is my name," he said. "What is it you want to ask me?"

"Did you know the deceased, Gabriel Birdsong, Mr. Jacobs?"

"You can just call me Carlton," he said. "Know him? I'm not sure I can say that I *knew* him, but I saw him around from time to time."

"What about his granddaughter?"

"That pretty young thing was his granddaughter?"

That was the first indication that Lena Birdsong had been in the house, but there was something in the way he said it that made me alert.

"You've seen her, but you didn't know she was his granddaughter?"

"Yeah, I've seen her a few times, but not much lately." He took another sip of coffee. "Mostly whenever I saw her, the old man was with her, and . . . well, they didn't seem to get along too well. Hardly like I'd expect them to act if he was her grandfather."

"Didn't get along? Like, arguing?"

He looked down into his coffee cup, his dark brow wrinkling. "No, not arguing, exactly. More the body language, like she didn't want to be near him. Of course, that could just be a normal teen reaction to being around old people. You know how teenagers can be."

I didn't know, in fact. Thanks to a truck driver who was either drunk, tired, or just not paying attention, I never got the chance to agonize over my son, Ethan's, teen years. But, you don't discourage the first person willing to talk.

"Yeah, know what you mean," I said. "When was the last time you saw the girl?"

He did some more of the wrinkled brow thing. "Must be a week, maybe ten days ago. I'm not sure. I think she and the old man were going to the store. That's the Korean food market two blocks west of here."

"Did they ever have any visitors?"

He shook his head. "Not that I ever saw. That old man wasn't exactly the social type."

You know when you've gotten to the bottom of the well. I had a feeling he'd told me all he knew, which came out to basically zero, or maybe a 'one,' what with the part about the girl and her grandfather not seeming to get along. That would be something I'd talk to my client about. I finished my coffee and stood. I took out one of my cards and offered it to him.

"Thanks for your time," I said. "If you should think of anything else that might be helpful, give me a call."

He stood, took the card, and placed it on the coffee table, carefully aligning the edge of the card with the edge of the table.

He showed me to the door, and stood there as I made my way to the sidewalk. Finally, the door closed. I found myself in front of the house next door to Birdsong's. The garbage container was still at the curb, missing its lid, making me wonder if anyone was home. As I approached the door, the dull boom of a radio playing too loud somewhere inside told me someone was home. I rang the bell.

And waited.

I'm a patient person, so I pushed the button of the doorbell again, and waited some more.

After what seemed like an hour—more like five minutes in reality—the door was opened. The blast of rap music that hit me was like a gale from a wind tunnel, and indicated that the door was a lot sturdier than I'd imagined. A surly looking, acne-pitted, light brown skin girl with a blonde afro and pink and orange polka dot eye shadow stood there, her boyish hip cocked to the right, a slender hand with pink and purple glitter nail polish on overly-long artificial nails planted on it. She wore a bright yellow halter top that barely covered her medium-sized breasts and orange shorts cut so her belly button was on full display. She regarded me indifferently.

"Yeah, what you want? We ain't buyin' nothin'," she said.

I flashed my PI card. "I'm not selling anything. Are your parents at home?"

"Nobody here but me and my mama, and she don't get home until 9:00 pm. What you want?"

If I'd been working a criminal case, I would've turned around and beat feet. The last thing you need is to have a perp walk because you questioned a minor without a parent present. But, I didn't think Constance Abel would complain, and there was always the possibility that another teen, and a girl at that, would know Lena Birdsong.

"I've been hired to try and find Lena Birdsong," I said. "She lived with her grandfather in the house next door."

She pursed her lips, then licked them. Her lipstick was a glittery purple, and not very tasty looking.

"You mean the little ofay chick who live next door with the perv? She missing? Say, you know he got offed last week. Somebody done cut his throat."

In a rush of words, with hardly a breath between any of them, she'd told me more than I'd learned from the previous two, even the cooperative Carlton Jacobs.

She told me that Lena did indeed live next door, that her grandfather aroused suspicion and revulsion in teenaged girls, that the people in the neighborhood not only knew what was going on, but talked among themselves about it, and that she herself was something of a racially biased individual. Of course, none of that was of much help in finding Lena Birdsong.

"Have you seen her lately?"

"Naw, last time I saw that bitch was 'bout two weeks ago. She 'n that old fart was comin' back from the groc'ry sto 'round the corner. That ofay bastard made her carry everything, too."

"Have you ever seen anyone visit them?"

"Naw, but then, I don't pay no mind to what other folks do, like, it ain't my business, ya dig. Why you lookin' for her?"

"Because she's missing, and her aunt wants me to find her." I could've taken the conversation further, but there didn't seem to be any point. I had a feeling I'd gotten everything useful from this one that I was going to get. I took out one of my cards and handed it to her. She looked at it, kind of squinty-eyed, and then tucked it into the left side of her halter top, almost dislodging her breast as she did so. "If you should think of anything else that might be useful, please give me a call."

"Sho, I do that," she said, and closed the door.

I couldn't exactly call that strike two. More like a high and outside ball.

I walked past Birdsong's house. The yellow tape had been moved from the sidewalk and walkway, but there was still a big yellow X of tape across the front door.

I stopped just beyond the edge of the tiny lawn and internally debated whether to check the house next door, or walk to the end of the block and make my way back. The coin flip indicated starting at the ends and working in, but, hell, it didn't make a whole lot of sense to walk down and come back. I was beginning to get the feeling that the only neighbors who might have anything useful were the ones who lived closest, and *that* wouldn't be all that much. People tend to think that it's New Yorkers who pay no attention to their neighbors. Those people have never been to our nation's capital. In DC, with so much of the high-income work force coming in from the Virginia and Maryland suburbs, and hightailing it out of the District when work's done, and the rest coming from the mainly low-income neighborhoods that circled the Capitol like stained beads on a cheap necklace, most personal relationships are income-related and confined to the office or shop. Once home, people mostly kept to themselves, and that was the ones who had jobs. The unemployment rate among the District's poor, mostly black and Hispanic, residents, is high. Those who wanted to work usually hung around a few scattered pickup points looking for day jobs at minimum wage, and those who were satisfied with unemployment or disability checks, hung with their homies near one of the hundreds of liquor stores that dotted the poorer neighborhoods, or stayed hidden in a bottle of the cheapest hooch they could find at home, on a curb, or in a vacant lot or alley. They kept themselves to themselves. In some of these places, the sound of gunshots or screams were only noted if they interfered with TV reception.

But, I was on the clock. Constance Abel was paying me to try and find—strike that, to *find*, her niece, and my grandmother taught me to always give a day's work for a day's pay.

I kept walking to the end of the block.

The house on that end was vacant, or so I thought from the plywood panels over the ground floor windows, and the gaping hole where a front door should've been. I was about to move on to the next house, when I saw a flicker of movement in the shadows beyond the missing front door. Someone was home. I walked up to the opening and peered inside.

An emaciated pale-skinned man dressed in tatters scuttled toward a dark corner of the vacant room.

"I ain't got nothin' worth stealing," he said in a weak, reedy voice. As I stepped across the threshold, he stopped, shrinking back against the wall. His rheumy eyes, just visible in the dust-laden light of the room, went wide. "Uh, hey, man, I ain't carryin', I'm just hangin' out here 'cause I got no place else to go." He raised his hands to his shoulders, palms out.

Damn, I thought, a homeless junkie. I doubt if he knew what day it was.

"I'm not the police, and I'm not here to rob you," I said.

"W-what you want?"

I stopped when I was about as close to him as I could stand. The odor coming from his body was stronger even than the moldy odor of an abandoned building, and it made my eyes water. Unfortunately, I was still close enough to also pick up the poor, stained teeth and stinky breath of a meth addict. The guy was a wreck. But, he was physically here, and might, just might, have seen something, so I'd ask him a couple of questions, tick that box, and get back outside where I could breathe the refreshing by comparison polluted air.

"I'm interested in whether or not you know the guy who was killed last week."

"Uh-uh, I didn't know him. I mean, I seen him around, know what I mean, but I never spoke to him or nothin'."

"What about the young girl who lived with him?"

"Yeah, I seen her two, once or twice. Nice lookin' piece."

Yeah, like he was ever sober enough to know the difference between nice looking and just alive. "Did you ever see anyone else at the house?"

"Naw," he said. Then, he blinked. "Well, there was this one dude, but he wasn't exactly *at* the house, know what I mean."

"No, I don't know what you mean. Explain."

He took a deep breath and let it out. The odor nearly knocked me off my feet.

"Well, he was like, hangin' out in the alley, know what I mean. Kinda lookin' at the house, through the windows, and stuff."

Interesting. "What did he look like, this Peeping Tom?"

"I dunno, just an ordinary dude, you know."

"Was he white, black, or what?"

"I ain't sure, 'cause he always wore a hoodie, but I think he's a white dude."

"Always, as in he was there a lot of times?"

"Well, I think I saw him mebbe, four times in the last month. I ain't sure."

"When was the last time you saw him?"

"Mebbe last week," he said. He began shaking. Whatever he was hooked on, he was in need of a hit. "I ain't sure, 'cause I was pretty wasted at the time."

His eyes were beginning to go out of focus. This well was running dry. I turned to go. No sense giving him my card. He'd probably have forgotten me within minutes of my leaving. But, he had added to my body of knowledge. Now, I had to find out who the mystery man watching the Birdsong house was.

"Okay, thanks for the info," I said over my shoulders.

"Hey, m-man, can you spare a five spot?" his weak voice asked.

Now, facilitating addicts is never a good idea, and I usually make it a habit never to give money to panhandlers I encounter on the street, but the guy did provide me some potentially useful information. At least, he'd given my investigation a new path to follow. I felt in my pocket. My fingers encountered some crumpled bills. I pulled one out, hoping it wasn't a twenty, breathed a sigh of relief when I saw it was only a five. I smoothed it out, turned and held it out to him. He snatched it from me like a starving man going after a loaf of bread, without even saying thanks.

It didn't matter. I was turning as soon as he snatched the banknote, and almost stumbled as I crossed the threshold into the cleaner, at least less evil-smelling, air of the outside.

After my lungs and nasal passages were clear, I resumed my trek up the block, hitting dead end after dead end—no one saw or heard anything, and knew nothing about what went on at the Birdsong residence, and at one house, the elderly Hispanic man who first opened the door when I rang the bell, slammed it in my face when I asked him about Birdsong.

I went back to my car, feeling as tired as if I'd just hiked a mountain trail in New Zealand. My inquiries hadn't really yielded any useful answers to the whereabouts of Lena Birdsong, and I was left with a new piece of the puzzle; who the hell was the mysterious hoodie-wearing stalker the meth addict had seen scoping out the Birdsong house?

Charles Ray

Chapter 10

Back in my car, I called Heather, and learned that Constance Abel had come, given her a deposit, signed a contract, and gone. I got her address, off a side street just over the DC-Maryland line in Silver Spring, Maryland, not too far from the Silver Spring Metro station. She had no recent pictures of her niece, but had, Heather informed me, provided a copy of her high school graduation photo, after warning Heather that she'd changed her appearance significantly since leaving school, so the picture probably wouldn't be much help. I got her phone number, and told Heather I wouldn't be making it to the office until well after lunch.

I called Abel and said I needed to talk. She wanted to know what about, but I insisted that it would be better if we discussed things face-to-face. She sounded reluctant to see me, which, considering it was her idea to hire me, struck me as passing strange, but I didn't say any of that to her. It does no good to do things like over the phone. You can't see reactions, so it's a wasted effort. When I confront people, I want to be able to see how they flinch, how their eyes flicker or squint, and whether or not they sweat. Body language says more than words ever can or will. She agreed, and offered to give me directions, but I'm pretty familiar with Silver Spring, so I told her there was no need, I'd find her.

It was easy enough to do. All I had to do was drive south to K Street, then west to Seventh, and north to where it turned into Georgia Avenue, and then follow Georgia out to Silver Spring. Her house was west of the metro station, which is close to the downtown area, just north of where the Walter Reed Army Hospital used to be before they moved it over and combined it with the Navy Medical Center in Bethesda, which now snarls traffic on Wisconsin Avenue all the way out to the I-495 Beltway during the week. In comparison, Georgia Avenue is a high-speed thoroughfare.

She lived in a tiny, one-story, red brick house, a cottage really, on a narrow street west of the metro station, on the very edge of the city. It was a quiet, neat neighborhood that looked to be populated by people of modest income, not quite poor, but not taking Club Med vacations every year either. I noticed a lot of older model cars of the type preferred by older people, easy handling, but lousy gas mileage, parked along the curbs. None of the houses had garages, although one or two had wide driveways in which they parked their vehicles.

Constance Abel's house had a postage-stamp-sized lawn that looked recently mown. Her walk was lined on both sides by neat rows of geraniums that were surrounded by a black mulch. Her concrete steps glistened in the sunlight, and the brass door knob was recently polished. I rang the bell.

She answered almost immediately. With her hair in a bun, and a white apron over her green dress, she looked like someone's grandmother. I almost expected to see a smudge of flour on her cheeks.

"You made good time getting here, Mr. Pennyback," she said. "Please, come in."

"Thanks, I'll try not to take up too much of your time. I just have a few questions."

I stepped into a neat-as-a-pin living room. Furniture arranged in neat groupings, white doilies on the arms of the sofa and chairs, and not a speck of dust in sight. Across the living room from the sofa sat an upright piano. On top of the piano was a group of photos.

"Would you like a cup of tea? I was just about to make a pot."

I'm not a tea drinker, but I was taught to always be polite. "Tea will be fine."

"Do you take anything in your tea?"

"A bit of lemon, if you have it," I said. "Otherwise, just black."

She went into what I assumed was the kitchen. There was a beaded curtain in the door, which rattled when she passed through it, but it closed too fast for me to see. I turned my attention to the photos on the piano.

There were several showing Constance at various ages, some just of her, and some of her with a man who looked to be a few years older, who I presumed to be her husband. I saw no photos of her brother, his son and his wife, of Lena.

I was so intent on examining the photos, I didn't hear her come back into the room until she spoke. "That is my husband, rest his soul. He was much older than me, but I loved him, and we had a good life together." As she spoke, she busied herself with putting a silver tray containing a teapot, sugar jar, creamer, and two fancy china cups on the kidney-shaped coffee table. She poured dark brown tea into the cups, and nodded at me to join her.

We sat at opposite ends of the sofa. I took a sip of the tea. The flavor was unfamiliar, but not unpleasant. She sipped her tea, eying me warily.

"I notice that you don't have any photos of your brother or niece," I said.

Her eyes flickered, and she darted a glance at the piano.

"Uh, Gabriel wasn't much of one for getting his picture taken," she said, holding the cup in front of her mouth as a kind of shield. "I had a graduation picture of Lena, but I left that with your associate this morning when I was at your office."

Sometimes when people want to withhold information from you, they don't talk. At others, they talk too much. I had a feeling that she was trying to avoid telling me something, and was using the cover of the torrent of words she'd just uttered to do that.

"Why was your brother reluctant to have his photo taken? And, why would you not have photos of your niece, such as when she was small?"

The eyes flickered again, and her hands trembled, threatened to splash hot tea in her face. She gingerly put the cup down. When she looked up at me, her expression was that of a small animal that has been cornered by a larger predator. No more 'flight or fight,' but the vacant-eyed stare of resignation.

"I don't really know why Gabriel was the way he was. He's, or was, six years younger than me, you know, and even when he was a little baby, I always thought there was something strange about him. It only got worse as he got older." She looked at me and blinked. "Whenever anyone pointed a camera at him, he would throw the loudest tantrums you've ever heard. By the time he was a teenager, everyone who knew him knew better than to try and take his picture."

"That must have complicated him getting a driver's license or a passport," I said.

"Not really, since he never had either. He also wouldn't pose for the school yearbook pictures, so, other than his transcripts, there's no record of his ever having attended school. He hated being noticed at all, and hated being around people. Pretty soon, no one wanted to be around him. The only person he ever seemed to like being around was Lena."

I couldn't explain it, but I had this feeling that she wasn't just talking about her brother's aversion to having his picture taken, but I thought it best to allow her to get around to whatever was bugging her in her own good time.

"Why don't you have any other pictures of your niece?" I asked, changing the subject.

Her expression darkened. "Her father and mother were . . . not very parental, if you know what I mean, they didn't take family pictures."

Probably too doped up to handle a camera.

"What about after they died?"

"Well, like I told you, my husband didn't feel that we could handle a child, he never really wanted children, so Gabriel got custody of her. He never let her get her picture taken. He didn't even know she'd posed for her high school photos."

Holy crap! This guy was beginning to make Scrooge sound like Mother Theresa.

"I'm surprised she didn't rebel. He sounds like a pretty strict task master."

"Oh, I think she might've had she been older when he . . . got her, but she was so young, and I traumatized by the deaths of her parents. He was turning her into a young version of himself, a total hermit. During school, I don't think she had even one friend."

Hell, this kid was traumatized from birth, with a couple of addicts as parents, and then being placed in the clutches of a . . . whatever the hell her grandfather was. She sounded like a good candidate for a therapist's couch.

"Based on her school picture, though, she's an attractive girl, Surely, she had a few friends, or a boyfriend."

"Oh no, Gabriel would never let her date. I didn't visit often, maybe once or twice a year, and he never came here, but I do remember when she slipped me the high school photo during one of my visits, she let slip that he'd never allowed her to date. She couldn't even go to her prom."

While I was processing this information, she stared down into her cup, as if trying to read some secret message in the dark brew. I don't know if she was even aware that her head moved from side to side in a kind of negative shake as she tea-gazed. Then, when she looked up at me, there was a strange expression on her face, one that, for all my experience reading body language, I couldn't fathom.

"There was this one boy," she said. "I don't think you could call what they did dating, really. He used to walk her home from school during her freshman year in high school." She closed her eyes. "I only saw him once, and that was the time when Gabriel found out about him. He was such a pathetic looking little boy, hardly bigger than Lena, and she was a tiny little thing. Gabriel caught them about two houses away. He sent Lena to her room, and lit into the poor thing like he was a thief or something. Poor child looked like he would pee his pants."

So, there just might be someone who knew the missing girl. "Do you remember the boy's name?" I asked.

"No, sorry, Lena would never say."

Damn, this was getting more frustrating by the second. How the hell was I supposed to find a girl who no one seemed to know, who had no friends, no driver's license, not even a telephone. I mean, what teenaged girl these days doesn't have a phone. I couldn't even be sure I had a decent picture of her. Who knows how she might have changed since high school? Not my client, it seems.

Ordinarily, at this early point in an investigation, I'd be making a list of what I knew, and what I needed to know more of, but since all I really knew was the missing girl's name, and I needed to know more of everything, it seemed a pointless exercise.

I spent a few more minutes grilling Constance Abel, and came up as dry as hole drilled for water in the middle of the Sahara. I thanked her for the tea and

Charles Ray

went to the office to see if Heather had been able to work any of her magic with the computer.

Chapter 11

Heather had *not* been able to work her magic, and was, if anything, even more frustrated than I was. It was as if Lena Birdsong didn't exist. The picture our client had provided had no markings on it, so we weren't able to determine what high school she'd graduated from, and Constance Abel didn't remember the name, just that it was in the District of Columbia— great, we could spend weeks contacting the high schools in the DC area, or Heather could spend days, snooping through their computer records, and both of us agreed that it wasn't an effective use of resources. So, after sitting at her desk, staring at me for half an hour while we tossed useless ideas back and forth, she suggested we knock off and hit it fresh the next day. I was up for that, so I went home early, arriving well ahead of Sandra.

After showering and changing into jeans and tee shirt, I went into the kitchen and started snooping in the pantry and fridge, looking for the makings of a special dinner. No, there was no special occasion, but when I'm frustrated by a case, I try to do something at home to keep the mood light so I don't infect Sandra with my rotten mood.

In the crisper drawer in the fridge, I found a head of iceberg lettuce that I didn't remember buying. The edges of the leaves were beginning to wilt, but it was still nice and solid. Underneath it was a plastic bag containing celery stalks that looked to be still fresh, and a plastic tray of medium-sized tomatoes, that I also didn't remember buying. Remembering my grandmother's admonition to never waste food, I took them out, opened the tomatoes and celery and dumped everything in the sink for a good washing. I put the sink plug in and ran the water until they were well covered, and while I let them set a while for some of the larger particles of dirt to wash off, I resumed my search. That yielded me a can of unsalted walnuts, a block of pepper jack cheese, and a large Macintosh apple with only one soft spot. Perfect, I reasoned, for a nice salad.

While I was washing, sorting, stripping, and chopping everything into bite-sized bits into a large wooden bowl, my mind drifted to Sandra, and how happy she would be that, left on my own in the kitchen, I wasn't whipping up a pot of my five-alarm chili with cornbread, which is, despite tasting like heaven on earth, not the healthiest meal for people on the shady side of fifty because I always sauté the meat in oil before adding the chili sauce, and I add an extra tablespoon of oil to my cornbread for flavor. Even though she likes it, and out of her devotion to me, eats a full bowl, she swears that she can feel her cholesterol rising as she eats.

Sandra and I have lived together for more than a decade. She finally made it permanent a few years earlier, when she sold her house in Takoma Park, an area of the District near Silver Spring, Maryland, and moved all of her favorite pieces of furniture and nick-knacks into the farm house we share just off River

Road, west of Potomac Village. While Potomac Village is one of the most expensive areas in Maryland's Montgomery County, with mansions valued at several millions, and gated communities behind ten-foot-high brick walls, the area where we live is where the countryside starts in earnest. My place was one of the last working farms that close in to all the wealth, until the old man who stubbornly refused to sell to developers, died and left it to his two sons, who had escaped the weather and politics of the Washington area for the zaniness of southern California. Not wanting to be saddled with a huge annual tax bill, and having missed the big real estate boom, they held an estate sale, and I got it for pennies on the dollar. In addition to the solidly-built house, complete with a large fireplace and lots of wood paneling, I also scored a big, weathered barn, which I use for extra storage and as a workout space. I keep my heavy bag, suspended from one of the rafter beams, where Sandra and I do martial arts workouts after our morning jog.

I haven't made many changes to the place. That's how well they built things in the 1930s. Except for replacing the kitchen appliances, many that looked they might have been originally installed when the house was built, and replacing them with gleaming, aluminum and white porcelain, top-of-the-line appliances, and reinforcing the exterior doors and adding alarms for the windows and doors, in response to a break-in when two thugs kidnapped me because I'd gotten too close to the art-theft ring they were involved in, I've left it pretty much as it was when I bought it.

It has a big front porch that we seldom use because the only thing to see from there is the winding, two-lane dirt track to River Road, and a roofed back porch that spans the width of the house. We spend a lot of time on the back porch when the weather's nice, because it gives us a beautiful view of the forest that makes up most of my backyard. The forest stretches down to the C&O Canal, and is home to an abundance of wildlife, including whitetail deer, foxes, badgers, squirrels, and more birds than I've been able to catalog. I've allowed what were once fields to grow wild, only cutting the grass in a rectangle around the house and barn out to about fifty meters. I learned that from my friend, Carlton 'Blood' Raine, a retired CIA agent, who lives in a fortified log cabin a few miles further west at the end of an unmarked trail a mile or two off River Road. It allows me to see anyone trying to sneak up on the house long before they're close enough to do damage with anything short of a rocket propelled grenade launcher. His theory is, if they're coming after you with RPGs, you've got a fight on your hands whether you see them or not, and the cleared space can work to their advantage because it doesn't interfere with their aim. I've never been attacked with RPGs, so I take his word for it. The man didn't get the nickname Blood for nothing.

I was working on autopilot, and by the time I heard the front door slam, signaling that Sandra was home from school, the salad was coming along nicely. It only needed a sprinkling of diced ham, which I'd already taken from the meat compartment in the fridge, and some bacon bits, and we were ready to eat. I was taking a package of bacon from the fridge—you didn't think I use the artificial stuff you buy from the spice shelf, did you?—when I felt the heat from Sandra's body against my back.

She slipped her arms around my waist and kissed me on the back of my neck. I almost dropped the bacon, not from surprise, I'd heard the brush of her bare feet on the floor, but from the electric shock of sensation her lips caused.

I stood, turned around, still in her embrace, and kissed the tip of her nose.

"You know, one day you're gonna do that, and surprise me, and I might turn around and give you a karate chop," I said.

She tightened her grip on me, rubbing her generous breasts against my chest. Man, that tee shirt felt like it was made of tissue paper. I could feel her nipples through it, her blouse and bra, and they were saying some pretty naughty things.

"Try it, buster," she said. "And, I'll squeeze until I crack a rib."

The thing is, she could. I've been teaching her aikido, karate, and taekwondo for years, and she's almost as good as I am. She's incredibly strong and athletic, and with her years of experience dealing with rowdy inner-city teens at Carter High School, is afraid of nothing.

"Hey, can't you take a joke?"

"Oh, joking, are we?" She ground her pelvis against me. "Say uncle."

"What do I get if I do?"

"What do you think?"

"Uncle," I said.

After one more pelvic grind, she released me.

"What are we having for supper?" she asked.

"I thought we'd eat light. A nice tossed salad, some garlic toast, and a bottle of beer. How's that sound?"

She closed those baby-blue eyes of hers, and sighed.

"Sounds perfect, only make mine white wine instead of beer."

"No problem, there's a bottle of Pinot Grigio in the fridge, right next to the beer. Why don't you grab me a bottle of *Tecate*, and pour the wine? I'll have this salad ready in less than five minutes."

She took a wine glass from the cabinet next to the fridge, and got the wine and beer out and, after searching the drawer in the cabinet, retrieved a corkscrew, and began extracting the cork from the wine bottle. "Are we eating in here or on the porch?" she asked.

"The weather today's so nice, why don't we eat al fresco?"

She poured a glass of wine, took a sip, sighed, and then passed me the beer, which she kindly opened first.

"Need any help?"

"No, you go ahead and get a head start watching the sunset. I'll be right out."

She grabbed the wine bottle, and went outside.

Less than five minutes later, I joined her, carrying a large plastic tray that held the salad, small bowls and utensils, a stack of garlic toast, and my beer. I set the tray on the small table sandwiched between two wicker chairs we'd picked up at a yard sale up in Clarksburg, Maryland one weekend, and dished out a generous helping of salad into each of the bowls. She, in the meantime, was pouring a second glass of wine.

We ate in silence. I noticed that Sandra really attacked her salad, and left her newly-filled wineglass untouched. We finished about the same time, so I took the bowls, utensils and uneaten salad to the kitchen. After putting the bowls and utensils in the sink, I covered the leftover salad with plastic wrap and put it in the fridge.

I grabbed a fresh bottle of beer, and went back outside, Sandra was just taking a sip of wine, looking over the rim of the glass at a herd of six deer that had just emerged from the edge of the woods. They were already looking a bit shaggy, which meant we were probably in for a cold winter.

"Nice view, eh?" I said.

"Yes, it is. I never get tired of just sitting here watching Mother Nature."

She looked like she had something on her mind. I debated whether or not to ask her what it was, knowing that she's a private person, and arguing internally to let her bring it up on her own time. I lost the argument.

"You look like you have something on your mind, babe," I said. "Want to talk about it?"

She blinked and flinched like someone who has been suddenly awakened from a nap.

"Oh, I do, but it's really trivial. We had a little incident at school today, and it's been on my mind."

"Was it that bad?"

"I suppose it depends upon your point of view. The vice principal, Mr. Carruthers, caught one of the ninth-grade boys trying to peek into the girl's locker room."

I pressed my lips together to keep from laughing. When I was a ninth grader, there was hardly a boy in my school who didn't try to get a peek inside the girl's locker. In our school, the two restrooms were adjacent to each other, and one of the twelfth graders even brought his father's drill to school, and drilled a hole in the back wall of one of the stalls, from which, for a dollar, guys could peek into the girl's toilet, with a narrow view of one of their toilets. I have to confess, out of curiosity, I paid my dollar too, but one look at a girl with a bad case of the runs sitting on the john cured me of peeping forever. Things now, though, aren't the same. What would get you sent to the principal's office for a good talking-to, or maybe a day or two of suspension, will now get you handcuffed and hauled off to jail.

"What's the school planning to do about it?"

"We're having a meeting with the principal tomorrow morning to discuss it. The problem is, the boy in question is one of our most academically gifted students. He's a bit socially stunted, but gets good grades, and up to now has never caused any kind of trouble. I'm just afraid they'll make the decision to report it to the authorities, and that will destroy whatever future he might have had."

That explained her mood. Sandra is one of those rare teachers who actually gives a crap about her students, often spending her free time, and occasionally her money, to help them stay in school and do well. It's how I met her. One of her gifted students, a young man with artistic talent, and a promising career, was gunned down in the street not far from where he lived with his grandmother. The police treated it as just another young black man falling victim to street gang violence, but his grandmother, and, I learned later, Sandra, disagreed. The grandmother hired me to find out what really happened to her 'baby,' assuring me that he'd never been involved with any kind of gang. I met Sandra during the investigation. She'd arranged for the kid, soon to graduate, to get a scholarship to college, and had often had him to her house, where he would spend hours in her backyard sketching the flowers in her garden. It was there that he'd seen her neighbor, and two men, transferring stolen art from a van to his garage. Unfortunately, he'd been seen as well, and to keep him from talking, the neighbor had ordered the two thugs—the same two who later kidnapped me and Sandra, planning to kill us and dump us in Rock Creek Park's wilderness—to kill the kid. He'd even tried to throw suspicion onto Sandra, claiming that she'd been having an improper relationship with the kid, a minor, and had had him killed to keep him from exposing her. When I confronted her about it, her response was to slap me across the kisser. Fortunately, this was before I'd taught her martial arts, or I might be wearing dentures today.

Things got sorted out in the end, though, and we discovered that, except for that initial misunderstanding, we were drawn to each other. We have a lot in common, too. For one thing, we both tend to side with the underdog.

"I sense you think this should be handled in-house, right?"

"Yes, I do," she said. "This boy's just painfully shy, but I think he's reached a point when he's experiencing thoughts and urges. If he's thrown into the system, they won't do a damn thing to help him, and it'll only get worse. What he needs is understanding, not incarceration."

"I couldn't agree more. Jail, especially for juveniles, is just crime college." I reached over and patted her hand. "Don't worry, babe. I have a feeling you'll be able to talk the rest of your colleagues around to doing it your way. You can be pretty persuasive when you want to."

She rubbed the back of my hand with her free hand. "Thanks, sweetheart. That makes me feel better. Now, I know why I keep you around. You're so good for my mood."

I did my best imitation of a leering seducer. "I'm good for a few other things, too," I said, which only produced a fit of giggles, and she snorted wine through her nose. "Oh, come on, it's not that funny."

She wiped the wine from her upper lip and blouse. "Sorry, babe, I wasn't laughing at what you said, because, you're right. You are *very* good at those other things. It's just that face you made. It was so . . . well, just don't give up your day job, because you'll never make it as an actor."

"So, you ready to go inside and let me show you how good I am?"

"Sure . . . no, wait." She snapped her fingers. "I almost forgot. I spent most of my lunch hour in the library. Remember I told you the name Birdsong sounded familiar? Well, I went through our old yearbooks, and I found her. Lena Birdsong was a student at Carter for all four years of high school."

"Wow, that's great. What're the chances of that happening, and of you remembering it."

"Well, you have to remember, there aren't that many white students at Carter. It's mostly black and Hispanic, so a petite, shy, white girl would stand out. It's just been so long, I'd forgotten about her."

"You knew her?"

"Just barely. She was very private and kept to herself. I think the reason I remember her at all is that boy."

"Boy? Her aunt said she never had a boyfriend."

A sad look clouded her otherwise angelic face. "He wasn't exactly a boyfriend. He sort of reminds me of the boy today, he was a loner, and if I remember correctly, quite a good student. But, he developed something of an unhealthy obsession with Lena." Her face screwed up in thought. "We didn't have that many white kids at Carter, even back then, or maybe, especially back then, so it was sort of natural that the two of them would gravitate to each other. Some of the other kids picked on them both, her because of her color, and him because he was, oh, what was the word they used back then, a dweeb. So, anyway, after they were teamed together in a science project, he began following her around."

Things began to make connections in my mind. "You mean, he stalked her?"

"Yeah, I guess that's what you'd call it today. Back then, it was just one of those teenage crushes."

Yeah. I'm not much for political correctness, but, there's only one way to describe what she was telling me, it just took a few tragedies for people to wise up and call it what it was.

"How did she react to it?"

"Well, she was a loner, like I said, and she had no other friends as far as I know, so she let him hang around for a while."

"Then, she broke it off?"

"I . . . guess so. I heard rumors, but have no way of confirming them. Anyway, after they'd hung out together for a few weeks, they started avoiding each other."

I think maybe I knew why they quit hanging out. "Do you think her grandfather might've had something to do with that?"

"Honestly, babe," she said. "I don't know. I never met her grandfather, who was her legal guardian. He never came to any parent-teacher conferences, or any school events, and she never talked about him, at least not the once or twice I could get her to engage in conversation. In fact, she never talked about her home life at all."

I could understand that. If the old man was as bad as his sister claimed, he'd probably forbidden her sharing anything about the family. I was more interested, though, in the stalker.

"What was the boy's name?" I asked.

She shook her head. "I don't recall, but I brought the yearbook for Lena's senior year, I'm sure he's in it."

I put my beer down. "What're we waiting for. Let's go look."

Chapter 12

The yearbook, a slightly warped 11 x 14 inch, leather-bound book, about two inches thick and in Carter's blue and gold colors, was poking up out of her purse on the couch. She pulled it out and shoved the purse over to make room for me to sit beside her. She started flipping the pages.

She'd been right about one thing, students with low melanin content were few and far between. There wasn't a student on the first five pages who wasn't black, or obviously Hispanic, except for two Asians, probably Vietnamese from the shape of their faces and their dark skins. Lena Birdsong, her dark blonde hair worn long, with a lock obscuring her left eye, was on the second page of students whose last names began with the letter B. I noticed that she was the only one on the page not smiling, and she was looking at something off to her right, rather than at the camera. From the hair style, the photo looked to have been taken around the same time as the graduation photo her aunt had left with Heather. She wasn't smiling or looking at the camera in that one either, although the lock of hair was behind her ear instead of over her eye.

After that, it was page after page of students of color, with just the occasional splash of non-color or Asian, who according to my friend Quincy Chang, don't like to be thought of as colored people. They're not white either, he said, but those living in the United States, seeing the way whites treated the darker races, chose to be in a category all their own. We'd almost reached the end of the book, when she stopped, her finger hovering over a picture. I didn't need her to tell me; it was him. This kid's photo could've been the illustration in the dictionary for the definition of dork. He had unkempt, brown hair that flopped over his forehead, touching his shaggy brows, wide, innocent-looking eyes, a broad nose with a lump halfway down the bridge, and a slightly protruding upper lip. He stared at the camera with an expression that reminded me of a trip I'd made to Phnom Penh, Cambodia's capital, from Bangkok, where I'd been working a case for Quincy's firm. I'd visited the *Tuol Sleng* Genocide Museum. The place, a former school, had been converted to a jail and execution center by the Khmer Rouge, who, like the Nazis in World War II, documented their atrocities with thousands of photographs. In S21, which is the designation the Khmer Rouge gave the place, there was a display of hundreds of black and white photos of prisoners, taken just before their executions, and some 14,000 of them were killed, either in the prison, or at the so-called Killing Fields on the outskirts of the city. All had a blank, resigned look, as if they had accepted their fate. The boy, Joshua Pearl according to the caption beneath the photo, had the same look. He looked as if the world had kicked him in the balls so many times, it no longer hurt, and he was just patiently waiting for the next kick.

I don't know why I knew. That's the way the brain works. It makes connections subconsciously, but I've learned to trust those connections, because they're usually right.

I'd identified my stalker, and it looked like he'd been at it for a long, long time.

Now, I had to find him.

Charles Ray

Chapter 13

The next morning, as soon as I got into the office, I briefed Heather, and set her to searching the Internet for Joshua Pearl. I wanted everything on him. After that, I went to my office and called Buster.

"Yo, bro, what can I do you for?" his booming voice echoed in my ear. He had caller ID on his phone, and knew how to use it. I was still working on just learning how to make a call without cutting it off on mine.

"I got a name I need you to run for me," I said.

There was a pause before he answered. "Is this for a case you're workin'?"

When I'm on a case, and dealing with a suspect or a stranger, while I keep it to a minimum, I don't always tell the whole truth. With clients, and friends, especially friends, I stick to the truth—or keep my mouth shut. On the phone, though, and when you've asked a favor, keeping mum's not really an option, so I told him about Constance Abel hiring me to find her daughter, and the problems I was having getting a line on the girl. So, I needed him to help me by checking to see what information the cops might have on one Joshua Pearl, a stalker in high school, and quite possibly the stalker one of the neighbors had told me about. That got his attention.

"That puts a different light on this case," he said. "I'll put that info in the file. You know, bro, there's only so much I can share with you on an open case . . . but, I'll let you know if there's a possible connection between this Pearl dude and your missing girl."

"Aren't you guys trying to find her, too?" It would be strange if they weren't.

"Yeah, but since she's over 18, we're not treating it quite like your ordinary missing person's case. She's a . . . person of interest."

"Hey, you don't think she offed her own grandfather, do you?"

Another pause. "No, not really. But, if what you say about this Pearl kid's legit, who knows. It wouldn't be the first time a kid did a parent in to run away with a lover."

That was sad, but too true. There'd even been a case in Northern Virginia where a teenager had convinced her boyfriend to kill her parents. Somehow, though, I didn't think that was the situation in this case. Again, I was trusting my gut.

"There's one other thing," I said. "It's peripheral, and a long shot, but could you give me whatever you have on the auto accident that killed her parents?"

"What? Man, that was a long time ago. It couldn't have anything to do with the old man's death, or the girl going missing."

"Maybe not, but you know me, I like to fill in all the blank spaces. It might help me understand her better, and that'll help me know where to start looking for her." Fingers crossed. That was a big maybe. I'm not sure why I wanted the information. At that moment, I was operating entirely on gut. I would soon have to get my head in the game. "Just call it curiosity. It's not a priority, but when you have the time, I really would appreciate it."

"Okay, that's not related to the current case, so there'll be no problem sharing it with you," he said. "But, we're a bit shorthanded right now, so it's gon' take a while before I can take the time to pull that old file."

"I know, amigo, and I appreciate whatever you can do."

I broke the connection, and sat back in my big leather executive chair. The leather was scuffed and it squeaked every time I moved. It was due for replacement, but my butt had worn a comfortable place in the seat, and I'd miss it. Maybe I'd let Heather pick one out at Office Depot or some other place, and then take a day off to allow her to junk the old one and replace it. That way, I wouldn't have to see what I'd come to regard as an old friend being consigned to the junk heap.

I swiveled around, shutting my mind to the squeaking protest of the springs in the chair, and stared out the window at the trees between the high-rise condos that squatted on the grassy expanses behind our building which, with their glossy glass and steel construction, not only blocked a lot of my view of the Ship Channel and the river, but in the late afternoon, the glare bouncing off their shiny exteriors made it impossible to look at the sliver of view that remained.

The view, or what remained of it, wasn't on my mind today, though. I was finally at a point where I could start to map out a plan of action, when I could start to put the dots down, even if I couldn't connect them all.

It hadn't been my intention to get involved in the murder case. The police are funny about that; they don't like civilians sticking their noses in police business, especially when it's an active homicide case. And, even though Buster was one of my best friends, if I stuck my nose in too far, he would be forced to punch it. But, it was unavoidable. Gabriel Birdsong's murder was connected to Lena Birdsong's disappearance, or vice versa. Whether it was because she was somehow involved and had run away, or had been a witness and was kidnapped, I couldn't be sure, but I knew that if I could get a line on why Birdsong had been killed, I'd be closer to finding her.

I didn't know a lot, and a lot of what I did know didn't make a whole lot of sense.

For instance, was Gabriel Birdsong's murder related to Lena's absence—I was still hedging on calling it a disappearance until I knew more—and, if so, how and why? Was Joshua Pearl the mysterious stalker, and if he was, was he involved in either the murder or the missing girl? Some of the things Constance Abel had said, and didn't say, were nagging at the back of my mind. Sure, she was quite forthcoming about her brother being a recluse, but there were unspoken words or thoughts that I caught from the look in her eyes as she talked about him. Was there some deep, dark secret in the Birdsong family closet that might have a relation to current events?

The case was like a moebius strip, it had no beginning or ending, just an endless loop of unanswered questions. The only way I knew to get to a point from which I could make some progress was to cut it. The problem was, where did I make the cut?

Charles Ray

Chapter 14

The darkness that wasn't really darkness, more a formless gloom inhabited by shapes and shadows, was no longer so intolerable.

She had finally found a position, seated with her shoulders braced against the dusty wall, that offered an almost-acceptable level of comfort. She'd even learned how to use the bucket placed nearby when her bladder or bowels became so uncomfortable, she could no longer stand it. She even got somewhat accustomed to the fetid odor of her own body waste, and was curious about the emptiness and cleanliness of the bucket each time she woke up from the dream-tormented session of sleep.

Sleep. She'd lost track of how many times she'd drifted away into troubled slumber. It could have been days, or even hours. Time held no meaning. She couldn't even tell from the food, fast food hamburgers and greasy fries wrapped in greasy tin foil, and sugary drinks of unknown flavor in stiff paper cups, without a straw, which she crumpled up and tossed at her feet whenever she finished gagging it all down. The trash, too, would be gone when she woke up.

Could whoever it was holding her here be putting drugs in the food or drink? That had to be it, she thought, because she was ordinarily a light sleeper, waking up at the slightest noise in her bedroom, a habit she'd developed over the years. The shuffle of feet dragging across the carpet of her bedroom had always yanked her from sleep. But, now, nothing. Just periods of sleep and wake, and she had no idea how long either lasted.

But, despite her inability to track the passage of time, her mind seemed otherwise clear—at least, it was when she was awake. She'd learned, for instance, to listen carefully until the only sounds she heard were the thumping of water pipes and the normal creaking sounds of a wood frame house settling as the outside temperature changed. Until she was sure she didn't hear the sounds that would indicate another person nearby. Then, she would hold her hands up to her mouth, and begin gnawing at the duct tape wound securely around her wrists, careful not to make big gashes that might be visible to whoever watched her when she slept. And, of that, she was sure. She didn't know why she knew; she just *knew* that as she tossed and turned in her sleep, there was someone there watching.

And, to her delight, the tape was now looser than it had been. She could even rotate her wrists, though only slightly. It won't be long, though, she thought, and this tape will be loose enough for me to slip my hands out of it. That, of course, was only one part of it. She still had the iron bands around her ankles, and the chain attached to a ring that was bolted into the wall.

Oh well, she thought. One thing at a time. First, get my hands free, and then I'll worry about the chain. Then, whoever you are, I'll make you pay for this. Oh yes, you will pay.

Chapter 15

Joshua Pearl, it turned out, was as absent from the Internet as Lena was. Heather could find no record of a driver's license or phone, and her contact at the Washington Metro Police informed her that a cursory search had revealed no record of arrests. I was surprised that they'd only done a cursory search, considering that I'd given his name to Buster, and he had to be at least a 'person of interest.'

I called Sandra at school, though, and she found the last address he'd given the school when he was a student, an address in Northwest, on a side street, two blocks north of Rhode Island Avenue, only a few miles from the Birdsong residence.

After lunch at McDonald's near the Waterfront shopping center, I decided to check the address out, on the off chance that he still lived there.

The address was a few blocks east of the Shaw/Howard University Metro stop on the Green Line, making it possible for me to go direct from Waterfront, and not have to cope with trying to find parking, which turned out to be a boon, because the narrow street had signs permitting parking for residents with stickers only. Not that I would've wanted to park there. It was a seedy neighborhood of town houses with steep steps leading up to tiny stoops with rusted iron railings. Many of the houses had broken windows and graffiti covered many of the walls. A few elderly people shuffled along the cracked sidewalks, some with shopping carts filled with detritus, marking them as the homeless who lacked the enterprise or desire to panhandle in the more affluent areas like Foggy Bottom or Georgetown, and men, some not so old, sitting on stoops with crumpled paper bags in their hands, which they lifted to their mouths from time to time, sipping the cheap hooch from the bottles inside.

No one paid me the slightest attention as I made my way from the metro station, except for a mangy-looking brown dog that, after running out of an alley and sniffing my shoes, followed me for two blocks before realizing that I had no food to offer, whereupon, it made a 'whuf' sound and darted into another alley.

I didn't look like any of the locals, or not much like one. I wore a pair of faded jeans and a brown knit shirt, under a light brown windbreaker. My shoes, brown hiking boots, were scuffed, but serviceable. I imagine I looked like a not-quite-so-desperate bum, looking for new hunting grounds, except that I was clean-shaven, and didn't shuffle when I walked. But, like everyone else I saw, I was black, which made me wonder why a white bread nerd like Pearl lived in this neighborhood.

Except for the lack of graffiti on the walls, the address Sandra had given me was not unlike the other town houses in the block. The red brick was stained by the exhaust fumes of the cars and trucks that rumbled down the narrow street, and a greenish-gray mold that spread like an abstract painting from the cracks between the bricks. One of the iron rails, the one on the left, was missing from the steep steps up from the sidewalk, and the concrete steps had spider web cracks, and looked like it might crumble under my weight. There were no broken windows, and neat off-white curtains draped over them on the inside. The dark green door had a brass letter slot, a tarnished round brass door knob, and a little arched window at eye level if you were an NBA forward. The button for the doorbell, a white plastic circle set in a brass plate, was just to the left of the door, in the cracked wood frame. I pushed it, hoping I wouldn't crack it further. A sound like wind chimes echoed from somewhere inside the house.

After a few minutes, a heavyset woman with medium brown skin and black hair, streaked with gray, pulled back into a severe bun, opened the door and looked at me. And, by look at me, I mean, looked me straight in the eye. She was my height, probably had twenty pounds on me, and had an expression on her face that could stop traffic without her ever having to blow a whistle or raise her hand.

"And, what you be wantin'?" she asked in a heavy Caribbean accent. "Whatever it is, I ain't buyin'." She fixed me with a stare from dark brown eyes that looked like they'd seen it all.

Slowly, so as not to spook her, or provoke her because she was holding a heavy-duty rolling pin in her hand. I gathered from that, and the apron cinched around her ample waist that I'd interrupted her as she was cooking, I reached into my shirt pocket and removed one of my cards, and held it up for her to see.

"I'm not selling anything, ma'am," I said. "I'm a private investigator, and I was told that Joshua Pearl lived at this address."

"And, what you be wantin' wit him?" She snatched the card and held it close to her eyes. "Mr. Al Pennyback?"

She hadn't really answered my question, I think, but she had the rolling pin and the weight advantage, so I thought it best not to mention that fact.

"I'm investigating a missing person's case, and he might have information that would help me find the missing person. Does he live here?"

She looked me up and down, inspecting me as if she was at the market and trying to decide which lettuce was freshest. I must have passed inspection, because she stepped back. "Well, come on in. I don't like standing and talkin' to no stranger on the stoop."

I squeezed past her into a narrow hallway that suddenly became quite crowded with the both of us occupying it. She turned and walked into a living room that was not much bigger. A large overstuffed sofa of some twill fabric dominated the room. It faced a large-screen television. Two small upholstered chairs flanked the sofa, and a square wooden coffee table sat in front of it. The wall behind the TV was covered with over a dozen framed photographs, some in color, most in black and white. She motioned me toward the sofa.

"Sit yourself down, and I'll be gettin;' you a cup of tea, and then we can talk," she said, and walked through an archway that was barely wide enough to accommodate her bulk.

What was I to do? I sat, idly staring at the wall of pictures. They seemed to be mostly teenaged boys, although a few looked older. A few looked like school photos. I was tempted to get up and take a closer look, but decided that would be rude, and this woman didn't strike me as someone who put up with rudeness.

I was beginning to think my coming here was a waste of time, and besides, I don't really like tea. That's more Heather's style. I like a good hot cup of Colombian coffee made from freshly-ground beans, no milk or sugar, just coffee, thank you. But, I'd force her tea down, make a little polite small talk, and leave. I had a case to investigate.

She came back carrying two dainty tea cups from which steam rose in a wavy column. The aroma of jasmine or some other flower preceded her across the room. Oh great, another of those flowery teas like Heather drinks. It's pleasant enough, but it has no kick.

She placed one of the cups on the coffee table in front of me and then lowered her bulk into the chair to my left, and blew on her tea. I picked my cup up and sniffed.

"It's hyacinth," she said. "Good for what ails you." She took a sip and sighed. "And, it taste good too. I put a bit of honey in it, and just a couple drops of lime juice."

I took a tentative sip, after blowing on mine. It wasn't half bad. In fact, it was pretty good. I took a larger sip.

"You're right, it does taste good," I said.

She gave me an 'I told you so' look and put her cup on the end of the table.

"Now, what you want to know about Joshua?"

Huh? Joshua? Did she know him?

"Uh, well, he went to high school with the missing person. I'm hoping that he might be able to help me find out where she is."

"What she do, run away from home?"

My initial instinct was to tell her everything, but I've been a PI too long to do that. I tell people I'm interviewing only what they need to know to answer my questions.

"I'm sorry, ma'am, but I'm not at liberty to discuss the case. Client confidentiality, you understand. Do you know where Joshua lives?"

"Sure, I know where he live, he live here wit me. But, I don't' know where he be hangin' out right now. He ain't been home for over a week."

Now, I was confused.

"He lives with you?" Stupid question. She'd just said that. But, the woman had that effect on me. It was like I was talking to my grandmother, but for the fact that this woman would make four of my grandmothers.

"What I just say? You got wax in the ears? Yeah, Joshua one of the boys that live with Mama Rosa."

Oh yeah, did I tell you, I'd forgotten to ask her who she was.

"Are you a relative, Ms. Rosa?"

She laughed, a deep, rumbling laugh that came from somewhere in her huge chest.

"You ever meet Joshua? No, you couldn't have, or you wouldn't be askin' that question. No, me and him, we ain't related, but I'm all the family he got."

I must have looked as confused as I felt. She laughed again.

"Okay," she said. "I tell you what you don't seem to have the brains to ask. Joshua's mama and papa died in a plane crash comin' from some conference in San Francisco when he was twelve. He didn't have no other family, so he was taken in by social services. I been a foster care provider for goin' on twenty year now, and since nobody else would take him, they placed him wit me. He been here since, that must be . . . eight year now, 'cause he just turn twenty last month."

"I take it you've fostered a number of boys over the years," I said, pointing at the pictures over the TV.

She followed my pointing finger, her expression a mixture of pride and sadness.

"Yeah, it I didn't have them pictures, I'd lose count. Some of them turned out okay, too."

"Joshua?"

Now, the expression was just sadness.

"Oh, that poor baby. He got more problems than Carter got liver pills. He never got over losin' his folks. He never come out of the shell after they went, and when he got older, he only got worse."

"What kind of problems did, does he have?"

Her eyes glistened. I hoped like hell she wouldn't start crying. I don't handle crying people too well, and one that weighs in the neighborhood of three hundred pounds is way out of my comfort zone.

She wiped at her eyes and took a deep breath. She'd regained her composure. I sighed with relief.

"When he was in school, it was just that he refused to make friends. He wouldn't join the school clubs or play sports like the other boys. They picked on him about it, but the teachers they took up for him, 'cause he was such a smart boy. Then, when he left school, he took to drugs. He can't hold a job, and mostly just hang 'round here watchin' TV."

Kids who do drugs, and kids who refuse to leave the nest are a pain to parents. I could only imagine what it must be like for a foster parent to have to put up with it.

"Has he ever been in trouble with the law?" I asked.

She shook her head vigorously. "No, he never done nothin' wrong, 'cept takin' drugs. He don' hang out with no bad crowd or nothin', he just get high and sit here starin' at the TV."

"But, you said he hasn't been home in a while. Where would he go?"

"I don' know, and that's what got me worried sick. He just a poor, skinny white boy that don' know nothin' 'bout the world. He ain't even got no friends I can call to help me find him."

"Did you have another foster child at the same time he's been here?"

"Oh, yeah, I had four of 'em, but Joshua, he never got 'long with 'em. They never fought or nothin' like that. He just never talk to 'em or pay 'em any mind."

"But, he must get his drugs from someone. Have you ever seen him talking to anyone?"

"Naw, like I done told you, he ain't never had no friends." Her eyes went wide. "Well, 'cept that one friend he had a while in high school."

"Who was that?"

"I never met her. All I know is it was some white girl. Let me think, what was her name . . . oh, yeah, Lila or Lorna—"

"Lena?" I prompted.

"Yes, that's it. Lena. He said she was gon' be his girlfriend. That's the only time I ever know him to have anything to do with anybody. Then, one day he come home all mad, and said this girl's grandfather had chased him off, and threatened to call the law if he ever saw him near her again. It done totally broke him up. I think that when he started doin' drugs."

So, Joshua Pearl and Gabriel Birdsong did have a history. That squared with what I'd already been told.

"Do you know if he ever saw her again?"

"I don' know. He was never much of a talker, and after that, he just shut up completely. Took to stayin' out late at night, and not comin' home straight from school. His grades dropped, and finally, he just dropped out right before graduation. Wouldn't even go and get his diploma."

Holy crap. This was one troubled kid. My mental list of prime suspects just got reduced to one person, and I had a feeling Buster's list of possible perpetrators for Birdsong's murder just got one more name to be added to it. Of course, that still left the sixty-four-dollar question: where the hell was Lena Birdsong?

I thanked Mama Rosa for the tea and the information, told her that I'd tell Joshua to call her if I found him—he'd likely be calling her from the DC jail—asked her to call me if he got in touch or came home, and left.

Charles Ray

Chapter 16

I met Buster for lunch the next day at Mom's. Over fried chicken, gravy, sweet corn, and corn muffins, washed down with several glasses of iced tea, I filled him in on what I'd learned about Joshua Pearl.

As I briefed him, except for an occasional nod, he gave no indication he was even listening; he never stopped eating. Except his diminutive wife, Alma, who rules the Mayweather household with an iron hand, the only things that can stop Buster eating are drive-by shootings, liquor store robberies, or someone messing with his car.

When I finished, he kept eating, he ate until the only thing left on his plate was a knife and fork, both of which he'd licked to get the last bit of chicken grease off.

"Okay, bro," he said, wiping his lips with a paper napkin. "Lemme see if I got this straight. This kid, Joshua Pearl, stalked Birdsong's granddaughter in high school after the old man threatened him and ordered him to stay away from her. A witness, and not exactly a reliable one, I might add, tells you that some dude's been watching the Birdsong house, and you think it was Pearl. So, I should add Pearl to the list of possible suspects in the old man's murder. Did I get it right?"

"Yes, except for the last part," I said. It amazes me that he can eat and still absorb that much information at the same time. "You just came to that conclusion all by your lonesome."

"Well, you tellin' me the kid's a doper kinda led me in that direction, or did you think it wouldn't?"

I looked away from him. "I thought him being an addict with a history of stalking, you might be interested."

"I'm interested, only because I got no other viable suspects," he said. "And, I hate to tell you this, but this kid's not lookin' all that good for it. Okay, okay, so he stalked the girl in high school. You know as well as I do that all most high school boys think of is pussy, so that's not gonna cut shit with the DA. He's not gonna bring an indictment on the word of a drug addict. As for the drugs, hell, the dude's got no record. All you have is the word of an old lady."

"You didn't meet that old lady," I said. I lowered my voice. "She's as big as Mom's, and twice as mean. Plus, she's been fostering teenage boys for twenty years. I think she knows when a kid's on drugs."

"That's a little strange, but not unheard of. Depends on what drug he's usin', and where he scores. We got a lotta white kids from the Virginia and Maryland suburbs get busted for trying to make a buy in the District, but even more of 'em get away with it. You're not really givin' me much to go on, old pal."

"If you could somehow tie Pearl to the Birdsong place, would that be enough?"

He shook his head. "The lab boys went over that place with a fine-tooth comb, and we ran DNA on everything we found, that's why we're lookin' for Lena

Birdsong. The only DNA they found in that place belonged to Birdsong, and to a female relative, who we assume to be the granddaughter. Funny thing, though, her DNA on a smear of blood on the toilet, which the techs say came from menstrual bleeding, and some skin cells and hair on the bed where the old man's body was found were the only signs of her presence in that house. I mean, knowing how messy most teenagers are, that's a bit strange, but that house looked strange, almost like no one really lived in it. Kinda gave me the creeps."

I was finding all this hard to believe. Not that I didn't think the DC lab buys weren't proficient, but they were looking for a killer, so I was pretty sure they confined their thorough searches to the entry points and the area around the body. I refused to believe that a person could live in a house as long as she did, and not leave some sign of their presence, no matter how small.

"Buster, so you think you could get me inside the Birdsong house?"

He looked hesitant, but then nodded. "Sure, I can do that. I think we've found all we're gonna find. You want me to go along?"

"No, you've got enough on your plate. Besides, I'll be going late tonight so I won't spook the neighborhood."

"Okay, go for it. I'll let the patrols in the area know, just in case your sneaky Pete shit don't work, and they spot you. In the meantime, I'll bet a BOLO out on Pearl. That satisfy you?"

I shrugged. "It's about as much as I expected. Thanks."

"Okay," he said. "Now, what say we try some of Mom's famous apple pie?"

Chapter 17

I told Sandra what I intended to do right after we finished supper. She didn't object, but I could tell from the look in her eyes, she wasn't thrilled about it. She never is when I do 'night operations,' although this one was pretty much a snap, a quick in and out, using an infrared flashlight, just in case, and night vision goggles courtesy of Blood Raine, my retired CIA friend, who had a nice stock of special ops toys thanks to his still-active agency friends. He let me borrow them anytime I needed something 'special,' on the condition that I give him a detailed field review of how they performed.

No other equipment was really needed, but I strapped my K-Bar knife to my ankle out of habit. You never know, the rats can get pretty big and pretty aggressive in a building that's been abandoned.

I waited until 11:00 pm to leave home, arriving in the area of Birdsong's house at 11:45. I parked three blocks away and hoofed it, carrying the flashlight in the leg pocket of my black cargo pants and the goggles slung over my shoulder. Dressed all in black, I blended into the shadows between the infrequent street lights, and probably would've looked like some skulking demon when I entered the cones of light, if there'd been anyone on the street to see me. But, the streets, this far north of the bus station, were empty. The hustlers, dealers, drunks, and dopers were further south, close to the bus station, Union Station, or downtown, and the rest of the neighborhood was either watching late-night TV or in bed.

I arrived at the house without encountering anyone. I could've gone through the front door, but thought it might be wise to go through the back. No sense getting reported by that one neighbor who happened to be looking out his window as I broke into the house.

I made my way around the side, traversing the narrow space between it and the house next door. The space was so narrow, I could hear the sound of the TV set blaring as I passed beneath a window, but no one cried out or challenged me. I was able to make my way easily by the light of the moon, and made it quietly to the back steps. The backyard was fenced in, but some boards in the wooden fence were missing.

Getting in through the flimsy door, which led into a small kitchen, was a matter of seconds. The old-fashioned bolt lock yielded to a little jiggling and steady pressure, and it didn't make much noise. Anyone hearing it might attribute it to a cat or dog prowling through the trash containers and junk that littered the backyard. That answered one question; why there was no sign of forced entry. A small child could've come through that back door. I wondered if the lab guys had come to the same conclusion, or if they'd even tried the door, and decided probably not, so I would have to pass that information along to Buster.

Inside the kitchen, I slipped on the goggles, and gave my eyes a few seconds to adjust to the green and black scene around me. I had to hand it to Blood and his spook friends, this was top of the line gear. It wasn't much heavier than a pair of designer sunglasses, and the resolution was fantastic. Except for the weird colors, it wasn't as disorienting as night vision goggles tend to be.

I did a careful quartering search of the kitchen, starting in the right corner near the door, and working my way around, peering into the pantry, cabinets, drawers, the stove, the refrigerator, and dishwasher. There was nothing there of particular interest, but what *wasn't* there was very interesting. In my admittedly limited experience with teenagers, and from listening to people talk on the metro, the one thing most teenagers have in common is that they do not eat the same things their parents do. The dried food in the pantry, and the limited fare in the refrigerator, seemed appropriate for an elderly person, but there was no candy, no sugary cereals, no nuts, not one single package of snack food of any kind. That, in itself, didn't prove anything, but I filed it under the 'unknown' category.

From the kitchen, I moved to the living room, again moving from the nearest corner and around the room, looking under and behind furniture, pulling open drawers, even flipping the curtains aside. Again, not a single sign of a teenager's presence. No fashion or entertainment magazines, no photos, no video games. One more item under the 'unknown' category, only now, it was also marked as 'strange.'

Next stop was the two bedrooms upstairs.

The larger, or master bedroom, with a walk-in closet and its own bath, took up most of the second floor. It had a king-sized, brass-frame bed that sat against the far wall, a large dresser and wardrobe chest, and bore the talcum powder, mothball, and sweat smell I associate with really old people. I eyeballed the room first just to get a feel for the layout. Nothing stood out particularly. It looked like I imagined a room belonging to an elderly person would look. I looked under the bed, in the dresser drawers, and the wardrobe chest. The drawers were mostly empty, and the dresser contained a boring assortment of tee-shirts, boxer briefs, two belts—one black and one brown—and socks. The underwear was all your basic white cotton, folded neatly and stacked so the edges lined up precisely. The socks were all black, and had been rolled and stacked as neatly as the underwear.

When I looked in the closet, I got a fuller picture of Gabriel Birdsong. He didn't have one suit or dress coat, just several pairs of pants, blue, black, and brown, hanging neatly and grouped by color, shirts, in white, blue, and brown, all solid colors, also neatly hung and grouped by color. At the very end was a faded brown windbreaker that looked like it had been ironed before being hung up.

What I saw was an unimaginative old man who liked things orderly, and was probably resistant to change in any form. He preferred basic, unadorned colors, which as I reflected on it, went along with the assortment of bland foods I'd seen in his pantry and refrigerator. This was a guy who would probably freak out if someone served him one of those multicolored kids' cereals, or put a sprig of parsley on his sandwich.

Of course, none of that told me where Lena was.

I did a quick check of the bathroom, and spent a few minutes looking in his medicine cabinet. Except for a container of aspirin, he had no medications, which was odd considering his age. I figured he'd at least suffer from arthritis, and would have some salve, ointment, or pills to treat that, but there was nothing. Even the toilet paper and towels hanging on the shower rack were plain white, and arranged in military precision. I made a mental note to have Heather check and see if she could find out if he'd ever spent time in the military.

Satisfied that Birdsong's master bedroom had told me all it had to tell, I left it and moved down the narrow hallway to the last room. It was at the end of the hall on the left, facing a door on the right, which opened to find a bathroom.

I decided to check the bathroom first, reasoning that it would be the one Lena used, but was surprised to find it bare but for the basics, tub with built-in shower, toilet, and a face bowl with a small mirror hanging over it. The mirror was one of those round jobs with an aluminum frame, just barely big enough to see your face in it if you stood at the right distance. Hardly what I'd expect in a teenage girl's bathroom. The toilet paper and white towel were arranged as neatly as they'd been in the master bathroom, and showed no signs of recent use. I checked the tub, feeling around the drain. It was bone dry, and little flecks of rust, some of which came off on my finger. It didn't look like it had been used in a long time. Strange. I checked the medicine cabinet. It was empty, completely empty. No medicines, no toothpaste or toothbrush, and no makeup. What teenage girl doesn't have makeup or acne cream? Didn't she even brush her teeth? Or, for that matter, her hair? I saw no comb or brush, just a sterile room.

Thinking maybe she kept things in her bedroom, I crossed the hall and entered the second bedroom.

A single bed, just big enough for one person to occupy comfortably, sat against the wall to the right. A blue blanket draped over it, and a single pillow with a blue case was placed atop the blanket. The bedside table had a small lamp, and nothing else. The only other furniture was a dressed with a mirror that was at least large enough to see your whole body. The top of the dresser was bare. I opened the drawers. Empty. Next, the closet. Empty as well, except for a bright yellow windbreaker, small, and I checked, it buttoned to the right, it was for a girl.

Where the hell were her clothes? Her personal items. There wasn't a photo, a magazine, not even a dog-eared romance novel. Except for the windbreaker, and the DNA Buster said the lab techs had found in the basement, it was as if she'd never been in the house.

I began getting a creepy feeling. The one place I'd yet to look, and the one place I really wasn't looking forward to, was the basement. But, it had to be done.

I made my way back down the stairs, and crossed to the door leading down to the basement.

The smell hit me as soon as I opened the door, the metallic odor of dried blood and the funkiness of dried feces and urine mixed in with the moldy smell of the basement, caused me to stop at the top of the stairs. The smell and the darkness got to me, but it had to be done. I felt around for the light switch, found it and flipped it. A single bulb hanging from the floor beams cast an eerie orange glow.

The stairs made squeaking sounds as I made my way down.

At the bottom, my shoes kicked up a small cloud of dust as I stepped off the stairs. I stopped and looked around.

The bed upon which Birdsong's mutilated corpse had lain was in the same place. The large, dark stain, from the headboard to the bed's midpoint was still there on the mattress. The sheet, I figured, had been taken by the lab techs for further analysis. The pillow, with the case missing, was now black with dried blood. The lab techs must've also taken that, although, I wondered what more they hoped to find on them. Unless the killer was injured during the commission of the act, all of the blood on both items came from the victim, and they'd found nothing else to indicate that anyone other than the old man and his granddaughter had ever been in the room.

At the foot of the bed was a straight back wooden chair that I hadn't noticed before. It was placed so that someone sitting on it would be looking at the bed. A rickety, one-drawer night stand was at the right side of the head of the bed, and on it was a small lamp with a flared, feminine-looking shade. The cord from the lamp snaked over the stand and was plugged into a double outlet on the wall behind the headboard.

In the corner beyond the bed was a two-drawer chest. On top of the chest I saw a half-empty tube of toothpaste and a much-used tooth brush, next to a brush, a comb, and a hand mirror. The creepy feeling started coming back. I walked across the room toward the chest, knowing before I got there what I would find, and getting more creeped out with each step.

I opened the top drawer of the chest. It contained underwear, bras and tee shirts, all small, all plain. The panties looked like something my grandmother would've worn. The second drawer was filled with neatly folded jeans, more tee shirts, a few blouses, and a couple of one-piece granny dresses. Everything was plain and had no personality, not at all what I'd expect a normal teenager to wear, but I was pretty sure now that I wasn't dealing with a normal teenager, and this definitely was *not* a normal household. Gabriel Birdsong's murder wasn't the only crime that had been committed here. My gut was roiling, and I felt like breaking something.

Chapter 18

Sandra was waiting up for me when I got home, even though it was nearly 2:30 in the morning. She took one look at my face, and pulled me into an embrace and just rubbed my back for several minutes, saying nothing. I would tell her, but later, when I'd had the time to process what I'd seen and what I was thinking.

I spent twenty minutes in the shower trying to scrub the smell of that basement off my skin, but I couldn't scrub the images from my mind. Finally, I gave up, pulled on clean shorts and a tee shirt and crawled in bed. I slid over until Sandra and I were spooned, and I pulled her close, and just nuzzled her soft hair with my nose, breathing her in deeply.

I held her that way until I felt her regular breathing indicating that she'd fallen asleep, and then I held on to her, lying there awake, unable to fall asleep. Three hours later, at 6:00 am, I gave up trying, and rolled out of bed. I tried doing it quietly so I wouldn't wake Sandra, but the movement of the mattress must have roused her. She groaned, and one bright blue eye peered at me through a tangle of blonde hair.

Our gazes locked. She must've seen the look of anguish in mine, because she blinked and pulled the pillow over her head. "If you don't mind, babe," she said in a muffled voice. "I'll pass on running this morning."

She knew I needed some alone time, some time to process everything. Then, we'd talk.

I padded to the closet and changed into my running togs, an old sweat suit from my army days which had seen far better days. It was so old, the gray had almost faded to white, and the knees of the pants and the elbows of the shirt were as thin as rice paper. Sandra pestered me often to throw it away and buy some of the new, trendy running gear, but my motto is, if it still runs, run with it. My running shoes, on the other hand, are fairly new. With my size twelves, and my five-times-a-week run through the woods behind my house when the weather's not too bad, running shoes have a short shelf life. I manage to get about three years maximum out of a pair. My new ones were Fila, gray with thin yellow stripes. I would've preferred a solid color, but I defy you to find athletic shoes that are plain these days.

After lacing my shoes tight, I tiptoed over to the bead and kissed Sandra's shoulder—her head was still under the pillow—and headed out.

The air was crisp, and the sun hadn't yet made its grand entrance above the tree line, so the sky was that odd shade of blue with pinkish tints. A few wispy clouds floated lazily overhead, and a lone hawk circled high over the trees to the south, no doubt looking for his morning meal.

I stepped off the back porch, took a deep breath, and started trotting toward the trees, spooking a squirrel that had been foraging for food in the grass just off the porch. It made a skittering sound and took off in large looping leaps.

The distance from the porch to the tree line, with my long strides, was eaten up in seconds, and then I was in the forest. I picked up the pace, pulling in air to fill my lungs, and then letting it out slowly, while my feet made crackling sounds as they pounded the dead leaves on the forest floor.

While it's not as good as meditation for quieting a troubled mind, running's not too bad, especially running in a forest that, even though it's close to the city, is dense enough to shut off the noise and make you feel like you're the only human being left on earth. There's a hypnotic effect from watching the gray-green and brown of the tree trunks as you zip by them, the dappled effect of the canopy overhead with the glinting points of sky that can be seen through the gaps in the leaves; from the sound of your feet on the dead leaves or hard-packed gray dirt, and your breathing as you suck air in and blow it out.

My normal morning run is four miles, two out and two back, which takes me almost to the canal. There's nothing magic about the four-miles. It's what they had us doing in the army before I retired, so I stick to it. I'm at an age, though, when I begin to worry about my knees and the effect constant running is having on them. Some of the guys I run into when I go to the Fort McNair Officers' Club for lunch tell me that a lot of people suffered real knee problems before the army got wise and started allowing soldiers to wear regular running shoes instead of combat boots, and stopped the ridiculous practice of making everyone run in a precise formation on streets and sidewalks. I'd retired before the jogging craze had really caught on. In special ops, we ran because we needed to be in shape for any contingency, and that often meant hiking, or if someone was shooting at you, running, for long distances carrying your gear. We never ran in formation, didn't wear regular combat boots anyway, and as far as I know, most of our guys didn't have the repetitive stress injury problems a lot of soldiers suffered. Not, mind you, that we didn't have a whole set of other problems.

The first two miles went by in a blur. Before I knew it, I was on the last little downslope before the ground leveled out to the canal towpath. I looped around and started back for the house.

There would be no wool gathering on this leg. The first half of my run is mostly downhill. The return trip, except for the last little spring from the edge of the trees to my backyard, is all uphill.

A hundred yards into the return run, and I was feeling it. My breathing was a bit more labored, and I could feel the burn beginning in my calves. Rather than slowing down, though, I picked up the pace.

The world constricted into a narrow tunnel of blue and green overhead, green, brown and gray to the sides, and a narrow rectangle of gray-blue in front of me. All I could hear was the 'thump,' 'crackle' of my footfalls and the rasping of my breathing.

The burning in my calves was on the threshold of being painful, but it was a bearable kind of pain, and I could feel a little stitch in my right side, where I'd once broken three ribs that hadn't set quite right, again, noticeable but bearable.

When I ran past that last line of trees and into the pasture that was my backyard, I startled a young deer that had been peacefully grazing. It gave me a wild-eyed look, made a 'huff' sound, angled away from me and in great leaps disappeared into the trees. I would've laughed, but I needed all my energy for breathing at that point.

At the back steps, I walked back and forth for three minutes to cool down and let the tension in my leg muscles ease. Then, I walked over to the barn, where I did ten minutes on the heavy bag, kicking and punching the crap out of it. Ten minutes of meditation, sitting on the hardwood planking of my back porch, completed my morning exercise routing.

And, I felt better.

The feelings of disgust and revulsion, the anger at what the things I'd seen in Gabriel Birdsong's house meant, were still there, but now they were under control. I could face them.

Starting with sharing them with Sandra. Maybe she could help me make some sense of them.

When I went in to shower and change, she was already in the kitchen, scrambling eggs in a big iron skillet. Four slices of bacon were laid out on a paper towel on the counter, and four slices of toast were stacked on a saucer nearby. She hasn't yet mastered the art of making fluffy buttermilk biscuits, and, in fact, doesn't really like cooking breakfast because of the effort involved first thing in the morning. This, I knew, was just her way of saying she knew that I was troubled, and she was giving me space and time to sort it out. I kissed her lightly on the back of the neck as I passed her. Neither of us said anything.

I went into the bathroom, stripped, and turned the shower on as hot as I could stand it. After a good scrub, I dried, shaved, brushed my teeth, and dressed for the day. Unsure just what I might get up to, I put on a pair of modified cargo pants, dark blue, with one extra pocket on each leg, a blue cotton shirt with long sleeves and an extra pocket on the left sleeve, and my black hiking boots. It wouldn't be appropriate for a business meeting with any of Quincy's clients, but should by some miracle, Quincy's firm had a job for us, I'd let Heather handle it. I was devoting my time and energy to finding Lena. I had a feeling deep in my gut that finding her would also yield answers to her grandfather's death. Nothing solid, certainly nothing that, as Buster would say, a DA would hang a case on, but the feeling was too strong to ignore.

When I got back to the kitchen, Sandra already had two plates on the table, and next to them, two cups of coffee, the smell of which had filled the kitchen. While I was showering, she'd also cooked hash brown potatoes. Unlike mine, which are hastily thrown together and often a bit lopsided, hers were perfect squares, three inches or so on each side, and a nice golden brown. If only I could teach her to make biscuits, she'd give Mom a run for her money.

I sat opposite her at the table, picked up my coffee cup, blew on it, and took a sip. She'd freshly ground some Colombian beans and added a touch of chicory like I like it. That first taste hit my tongue, burning a little, but oh so good as the hint of sweetness of the chicory combined with the rich, dark earth taste of the coffee made love to my taste buds. There are two things that top my list of enjoyment—well, three if you count sex—the first beer on a hot day, and the first cup of coffee in the morning.

"That's perfect," I said, putting my cup down and picking up a fork. "If you ever learn how to cook biscuits, I'm gonna have to lock you up here, because every restaurant in town will be trying to hire you as head chef."

She smiled at me over the rim of her cup. "You're just saying that because it's true."

"If only I could teach you to make a decent biscuit."

She frowned. "I don't understand it," she said. "I use the ingredients from the cookbook, in the exact amounts, but my biscuits still turn out like hockey pucks. I just don't know what I'm doing wrong."

I wasn't about to say I agreed with her, but I did. One of her biscuits, thrown hard enough, could knock a man on his ass.

"Maybe that's the problem. You're following the recipe book."

"You don't?" Her eyes were wide. "But, yours are always so fluffy. How do you do it if you don't have a recipe?"

"I do, but it's up here." I tapped my temple. "My grandmother taught me how to bake buttermilk biscuits when I was, oh, eight or ten, and she could barely read. She didn't even own a recipe book."

"So, what's the big secret?" She had a skeptical look on her face. "You put some secret herb or spice in your dough?"

I couldn't help but laugh then, but I stopped when she frowned. "Okay, okay," I said. "The secret, well, the secrets, are to add egg to the dough, and don't knead it too long. The egg adds body and flavor, and if you only knead it once or twice, and dust it lightly with flour, the biscuits come out fluffy. If you knead them too much, it increases the gluten, which is what makes them hard." Of course, I learned all that long after leaving home. My grandmother didn't know what gluten was, and probably didn't care, but she did like her biscuits fluffy.

"Well, aren't you just a font of knowledge. Who would ever think that a hard-nosed special operations commando would also be a master chef?"

"What can I say? I'm a multi-talented guy."

She winked at me and leered. I knew which of my many talents she was thinking of at that moment, and expected her to make some off-color, suggestive comment. But, she surprised me.

"You ready to talk about it?" she asked.

I didn't need her to explain what *it* was. I knew. And, I also knew that she'd been easing me along, setting me up so that I would feel at ease. The woman's as much of a magician with people as Heather is with computers.

"Yeah, I guess I do need to share it with someone," I said, and then I told her what I'd found, and what I thought it meant.

She didn't look shocked exactly, more kind of disappointed. "Do you really think Gabriel Birdsong was abusing Lena, his own granddaughter?" She already knew what I thought. I think she just wanted me to repeat it, so she could be sure.

"The signs are all there," I said. "I don't know if it was . . . sexual, but it does look like he kept her pretty much in the basement, and then there's his not allowing her to have friends. From the look of his bedroom and kitchen, in addition to being a recluse, the guy was some kind of control freak."

She began playing with her food, stirring the eggs around the plate, and then making a little pile of them atop one of the hash brown squares.

"I suppose we should've seen the signs when she was in school," she said. "But, other than her always going straight home from school, and not having any friends, there were no signs of . . . abuse of any kind. I mean, she never even gave a hint."

"Hey, don't beat yourself up, babe. The cops scoured that place after the old man was killed, and they didn't notice anything either. Of course, they were focusing on the murder, so they pretty much just looked for evidence around the bed where he was clearly killed, and the doors and window to see if someone might've broken in. I went through drawers, closets, everything, and I wasn't looking for a killer, I was looking for signs of the girl, so my judgment wasn't clouded by a preconceived notion of what I might find. And, I'm not sure, it's just a gut feeling. The way the house looked, along with bits and pieces that people, you included, have told me since I started this damn investigation."

"I know you're right, Al, but I still feel responsible. When kids are maltreated at home, school's just about the only safe haven left, and when we fail, well . . ."

"You didn't fail. Sometimes, bad shit just happens."

"You will find her, won't you?"

Would I? If I did, would it be in time? Or should I even try? Damn right, I should, and I would.

"Yeah, I'll find her."

That calmed her, and we finished the rest of our breakfast in a slightly upbeat mood. She left for school first, and after cleaning the kitchen, I jumped in the bug, and headed for the office.

Buster, dressed in jeans, and a Redskins sweatshirt, was waiting for me in the office. He was sitting in the chair at the side of Heather's desk, sipping some of her flowery tea. They both smiled when I pushed through the door.

"Hey, bro, keepin' banker's hours I see," he said.

I looked at my watch. It was 7:59. "I'm not on a clock," I said. "Besides, I worked real late last night."

He looked at me through narrowed slits. "Oh yeah, I forgot. You find anything you want to tell me about?"

"I did. You two want to come into my office, and after I've had my second cup of coffee, I'll fill you in."

"You better put that coffee in a travel mug, bro," he said. "That is, unless you don't want to go with me when I execute a search warrant on Joshua Pearl's place."

"I think I'll have that coffee when we come back. Let's go."

I preceded him out the door and down to the parking lot, where I headed for my car.

"Hey, bro," he said. "Why don't you ride with me. You can brief me on your little night raid while we drive. Don't worry, I'll drop you back here when we're done."

I was up for that. I hadn't actually been looking forward to looking for parking. I walked to one of our guest slots, where he'd parked his car, not actually *his* car, but a nondescript brown Crown Victoria, which I guessed was an official undercover vehicle he used when he went out on calls, or served warrants. Or, maybe he just didn't want to take his shiny new car to

Pearl's neighborhood, which was a sentiment I could agree with.

I slid into the passenger side and fastened the seatbelt. He got behind the wheel and did the same. Expertly, he backed out, and knocked up gravel as the souped-up engine of the Crown Vic roared, and we were on our way.

Buster drives like he eats, with gusto. I had the padded dash in a death grip as he wove through traffic, going up Fourth Street and right on N Street, where he did an illegal left turn onto South Capitol Street., causing oncoming traffic to skid to a stop with much blowing of horns and jabbing of middle fingers at us. We went around the Capitol Building and took First Street to Union Station, and then Massachusetts Avenue to Seventh Street, where he turned north until we reached the intersection not far from the Shaw Metro station and to the narrow street where Mama Rosa's house was. He parked directly in front of the address, shut the engine off and sat there staring at the building.

"What are we waiting for?" I asked.

"Is this Mama Rosa really as big as Mom?"

"Yup, and twice as intimidating."

"In that case, you go first. You've met her already, so it won't be as much of a shock as it would be if she opens the door and a cop's standing there with a search warrant."

As hard as I tried—well, maybe I didn't really try too hard—I couldn't keep from laughing, which caused him to glare at me. "So, that's why you wanted me to come along. You're afraid of a woman."

He glared even harder. "I am not," he said, but without conviction. "I just want things to go smoothly. Now, get your ass up there and ring the damn bell."

I was still chuckling when I got out of the car and went up and rang the doorbell.

Mama Rosa's face lit up in a big smile when she opened the door and saw me there smiling like an idiot.

"Well, if it ain't Mr. Al Pennyback. You come back for some more of Mama Rosa's tea?"

I stepped aside to let her get a look at Buster, who had followed a couple steps behind me. Her smile turned to a look of puzzlement, and then changed into a frown.

"Why you bring police wit you, eh?" Her eyes went round like saucers. "Is something wrong wit my Joshua?"

Buster stepped forward, his badge held up in his right hand, and the search warrant in the left. "No, ma'am," he said. "At least, not as far as we know. We . . . we're looking for Joshua Pearl in connection with a case we're working on. What I have here, ma'am, is a search warrant that allows me to search his room. I assume that he has a room of his own?"

She blinked and looked at me. "This got to do wit that girl what you lookin' for?"

I shared a look with Buster. He nodded slightly. "Yes, ma'am," I said. "She and your, Buster, were friends in high school. We're hoping he might be able to help us find her."

"But, how is searchin' his room gon' be helpin' you do that?"

I knew that Buster had gone along with making it seem as this was part of my case because it was easier than telling the woman we considered her ward a possible murderer, but now, he looked flustered. Things could go sideways if we told her the real reason now, she wouldn't trust me anymore, and for reasons I couldn't understand, that thought bothered me.

"You know how it is, Mama Rosa," I said. "Teenagers take pictures, share mementos and stuff. We're hoping maybe Joshua has something belonging to Lena, that's the missing girl, that might help us find her. It might help us find him, and he might even know where she is."

She looked at me so long, I wasn't sure she bought the bullshit story I'd just spun for her. I noticed that Buster was holding his breath. Finally, she smiled.

"Yeah, these kids just like pack rats, that's for sure. Okay, you go on and look through his room. It's the first on the right at the top of the stairs. If you need to look at any other part of the house, you go right ahead, 'course, Joshua, he only stay in his room, and sometime hang out on the sofa watchin' TV. I go make some tea." She looked at Buster. "You like jasmine tea, Mr. Policeman?"

Buster let out his breath. "Yes, ma'am," he said. "Jasmine tea sounds great."

"Good. I put a little honey and lemon in it. You like a man what like sweet stuff."

She stepped back and let us enter. After pointing to the stairs, she waddled off to the kitchen. Buster looked at me, relief and confusion warring for space on his brown face.

"Jasmine tea? She's kidding, right?"

I shook my head. "No, she's not kidding, bro. But, it actually tastes okay."

He shivered and turned for the stairs. I followed.

The door to Pearl's room was ajar. Buster tensed as he pushed it open, and slowly entered, his gaze sweeping from left to right and his hand not far from the 9mm automatic he had strapped to his waist. I came in close behind him. My senses told me the room was empty, and no one had been in it for a while. The smell was what you'd expect from a drug addict, sweat and some other musty odor hung heavy in the air. It looked like I'd expect a teenage boy's room to look, clothing strewn all over the place, and most of it in need of a good washing or two. But, the smells were all old. The smell was horrible, but old.

Buster reached in his rear pocket and pulled out a pair of surgical gloves and handed them to me, then he took out another pair and pulled them on.

"No way in hell I'm touchin' anything in here with my bare hands," he said, and I knew he didn't mean for fear of contaminating evidence.

I pulled my own gloves on.

"So, how do we go about doing this?" I asked. "You want me to take the drawers, and you do the closet?" I pointed to the closet door in the corner opposite the entrance door.

He looked down at the clothing scattered around. "Yeah, but I think we oughta check the pockets in the junk on the floor." He walked to the wall opposite the bed and pointed toward the foot of the bed. "I'll start over here, and you do the stuff around the bed."

He looked about excited at the prospect of touching the filthy garments as I felt, but it had to be done. I knelt, and gingerly poked at the pocket area of jeans and trousers, many smelling of dried urine and something a bit gamey, feeling nothing strange. Behind me, I heard Buster snort and make a derisive sound.

"Nothin' over here," he said. I stood and watched him stand and stretch his back.

"Same here," I said.

"Okay, you do the drawers, and I'll check the closet."

The large, three-drawer dresser was to the left of the door. I kicked aside a pair of crumpled jeans as I approached it. On top of the dresser, there were a couple of unopened packs of cigarillos. Next to them was an open pack. One of the tiny brown cylinders lay atop it next to a knitting needle. I remembered something I'd read somewhere about drug addicts inserting their desired opiate into cigars, usually strong-smelling ones, which enabled them to toke up in public. I wondered what Joshua Pearl stuffed into his cigarillos. The only other thing on top of the dresser was a crumpled and faded dollar bill.

Gingerly, I opened the top drawer. It contained tee shirts, briefs, and socks in various colors and styles, some folded, some just sort of crumpled up. There was no order to the drawer. Things had just been crammed in wherever they would fit. I carefully pulled items out, inspecting underneath them, worried that he might have a supply of his knitting needles stored in the drawer. My surgical gloves wouldn't protect me against that.

After turning up nothing interesting in the top drawer, I closed it and eased the second one open.

This one contained polo shirts and tee shirts, many with rock band logos. Because they were larger and harder to just stuff in a drawer, it wasn't quite as messy as the underwear drawer above it. That, of course, is relative. It was still chaotic. I lifted each shirt out, inspecting the pockets of those that had them, and stacked them on the floor.

I struck pay dirt at the bottom of the second pile.

The 9 x 13 brown envelope was crinkled and torn in places. The flap was tattered from being opened and closed many times. And, it bulged out in places. I grasped it by the corner, lifted it out of the drawer and put it on the only clear space there was on top of the dresser.

I peeled back the flap and lifted the edge to get a look at the envelope's contents.

Photographs, mostly in color, four inches by five inches, some creased and torn at the edges, were crammed haphazardly inside. I held the envelope by the bottom and tilted to let them slide out onto the top of the dresser.

Moving them carefully to avoid smudging any fingerprints that might be on them, I began spreading them out on the dresser top. Each photo was of Lena Birdsong, most of her alone, but a few showing her with her grandfather in the backyard of their house. Blurred edges of leaves, limbs, and in a few cases what appeared to be the top of a wooden fence, indicated that the girl and her grandfather had been photographed from hiding.

"Damn," I said.

Buster jerked back from examining the ratty looking garments hanging unevenly on the closet rack.

"What is it?" he asked.

"Come here. You've got to see this."

He walked over and looked down at the dozen or so photos I'd spread out. "Holy shit. The little turd *was* stalking her."

"Yeah, and from the changes in foliage and the clothing they're wearing in different pictures, I'd say over a long period of time," I said.

He nudged me aside and began scooping the photos back into the envelop.

"Let's get the hell out of here," he said. "I got myself a whole new case."

Charles Ray

Chapter 19

Before taking me back to my office, Buster swung by his precinct. He had me sit in a chair near his desk, which was usually reserved for perps being interviewed or just about to be carted down for booking, while he hit the phone and yelled instructions to the detectives under him. His desk was at the back of a big room that served as the bull pen for the detectives assigned to the precinct, a space crowded with rows of desks which, except for his as a supervisor, were arranged in groups of two, so that the detectives worked in pairs facing each other. Off to the left side of his desk, against the wall, was a large cork board upon which he'd had one of the detectives pin the photos we'd found in Joshua Pearl's room.

My eyes kept straying to the pictures, fifty-three in all, arranged in semi-neat rows against the medium cork surface.

"Mahoney," Buster said in a barking voice. "I want you to get an APB out on Joshua Pearl."

"Sure thing, boss," a sandy-haired detective with a receding hairline and a growing paunch said. "What's he wanted for?"

Buster screwed up his eyes in concentration. "Make it, wanted for questioning in connection with the death of Gabriel Birdsong, and the disappearance of his granddaughter, Lena Birdsong," he said finally.

"Damn, you think he did it?"

Buster glanced at the photos.

"I'm not sure at this point, but he fucking well has a few questions to answer."

Mahoney nodded and rushed off to do whatever he had to do to get an all point's bulletin issued. When he was gone, Buster shuffled some papers on his desk and mumbled something unintelligible.

"You really think Pearl killed the old man?" I asked.

He looked at me and blinked as if he'd forgotten I was there. Given all that had to be going through his mind, it's a good chance he had forgotten.

"You found those photos, you see 'em. What do you think? The dickhead's been stalking that girl for who knows how long. He's clearly obsessed with her. So, yeah, I think he did it, and I think he took her and has her stashed away somewhere."

Maybe I looked skeptical, or maybe it was just to get his thoughts out into the open, but Buster rose from behind his desk, walked to the photos and held a huge hand up toward them.

"Look," he said. "This is proof positive that the kid was stalking the girl, so your drug addict informant got that right." He turned to face me dead on. "Here's how I think it went down. He watched her for months, and finally worked up the nerve to put a move on her. The old man caught him and confronted him, and he slit his throat."

It could've gone down that way. But, some of the facts of the case argued against that scenario.

"But, these photos are all taken outside. If it went the way you said, how'd the old man get undressed and in the basement?"

"Hey, the kid's a perv. These pictures prove that. Maybe he drug the old coot down afterwards."

"Nope, won't wash. The amount of blood in the basement, and the splatter pattern indicates he was killed there, probably right where he was laying."

"Shit, I don't know, bro. Maybe he knocked him out, drug him down and did him. However the fuck he did it, as far as I'm concerned, Joshua Pearl's good for this, and I think he kidnapped your girl. So, we find his ass, we solve both cases, yours and mine."

Easy peasy, and all wrapped up with a nice red bow. Only, I wasn't buying it, and, it's not because I'm a contrarian. Something just didn't fit. I didn't know what that something was, but it did not fit. My eyes kept being drawn to those damn pictures. Something about them nagged at me.

Then, it hit me. In every one of the photos, even the ones where she was with her grandfather, Lena Birdsong was not smiling. Sure, she hadn't smiled in her school photo either, but I don't know anyone who goes through life with the same forlorn look on their face one hundred percent of the time. You'd expect, alone in her backyard, as she was in most of the photos, even if she didn't smile, she'd have another expression on her face. But, no, she had that same deer-in-the-headlights look, almost a grimace, in each and every photo. In the ones where the grandfather was present it was, if anything, more pronounced.

No, this case was not as cut and dried as I'm sure Buster's police mind wanted it to be. Something else was going on.

And, I was determined to find out what.

Charles Ray

Chapter 20

At first, she didn't realize that she was dreaming. The dream was so real. At the same time, it was extremely . . . unreal.

She felt rather than saw the dark shape looming over her, but the smell, like the back of a musty closet, was strong in her nose, that, and the smell of sweat. She writhed and tried to back away, but her arms and legs wouldn't respond to her commands to move.

The hands that roamed roughly over her body were calloused and sweaty. They probed her in places that other hands should never touch. She tried to pull away, but there was nowhere to go.

Then, she felt the weight, and the dark shadow blocked out everything. She felt her legs being pried apart. The pain, when it came, was like a white-hot poker being stabbed into her body. The weight felt as if it would suffocate her. Her breathing was labored, and the pain intensified.

"No, please, no," she said, but a calloused, sweaty hand clamped over her mouth, cutting off her plea.

Her body bucked, trying to throw the weight off, but it only pressed down harder.

Finally, realizing that her struggles were not helping, she let her body go limp. She could hear a hoarse grunting, and the odor of stale tobacco and onions almost made her gag. She swallowed to keep the bile down, somehow knowing that if she vomited, it would only get worse. She didn't know how she knew this—somehow, though, she thought she should know.

After what felt like an eternity, the weight lifted. The pain at the junction of her legs, though, remained, now just a dull ache. She felt something hot and sticky on her legs and stomach, and almost gagged again. For the last few minutes of her ordeal, she'd kept her eyes tightly shut. Now, she opened them. Everything was fuzzy, but she could see the dark shadow shambling away from her, toward a far corner of the room, wherever that room was—she didn't know.

That's when she screamed.

"No, no, no-o-o-o-o-o-o!"

She heard a dull knocking sound, and felt a new pain in the back of her skull.

Then, she snapped awake. But, she still heard the knocking sound, and the pain in her head was sharper. Most disturbing, though, was the screaming. She could still hear it. She flung her head from side to side. The knocking stopped, but not the pain, and she realized with a start that the screaming she heard was coming from her own mouth.

She was scrunched against the wall of the basement. Sweat poured from her brow and into her eyes, stinging like hell. She stopped screaming.

Slowly, the turmoil in her mind receded. She realized that she'd been dreaming, and she'd had a nightmare. She'd been knocking her head against the basement wall.

The duct tape was still around her wrists, albeit a bit looser now that she'd been working at it for some time. The metal bands were still tight around her ankles.

She was still being held prisoner in some damn basement. She had to get out. She *would* get out, and she'd make whoever did this to her pay, and pay dearly.

"Let me out of here, you son of a bitch," she yelled. "You stinking pussy, are you afraid to face me? Get your ass in here and talk to me. Do you hear me?"

But, no one answered her.

Charles Ray

Chapter 21

I'd considered sharing my suspicions with Buster, but I didn't think he'd be in a mood to listen to what was a pretty crazy theory, unsupported with anything but my gut feelings.

I was neither surprised, not particularly disappointed by the way he was thinking. He was doing what cops do, trying to close a case. Now that he had a viable suspect, and evidence linking him to the crime scene, he would pull out all the stops to find him and put him away. I suppose, in his place, I might do the same thing.

Hell, I was having something of a hard time really convincing myself. My gut, feeding off my lizard brain and millions of years of evolution were telling me one thing, but that rational part of my mind, the part that, after all our civilizing over the centuries tries to keep the lizard brain caged up, wasn't at all sure that I'd read things right.

It didn't help that it was late on a Friday afternoon, and I was sitting in my office, leaning back in my chair gazing up at the spider-web cracks in the ceiling, while Heather continued to peck away at her keyboard on the other side of the door, unaware of my angst. I'd considered sharing my thoughts with her, but decided against it. I didn't want anything interfering with her search for information. If I told her what I was thinking, she might go off on a tangent to verify my suspicions and miss something important. I couldn't tell Buster, because he'd ask for evidence, not gut feelings, and I didn't really have any hard evidence.

I looked at my watch. 4:45. Close enough, I thought. I slumped forward, stood, and shoved my chair back, banging it against the wall. Might as well go home.

Heather was hunched over her computer, concentrating on something on the screen, when I exited my office.

"Hey, kiddo, I'm calling it a week," I said. "You ought to close up shop and go home."

She turned her head and looked at me through a stray fringe of hair. "I'll go in a few minutes. I'm just tracking some information on this guy, Joshua Pearl. I finally found a few hits on him."

"Anything useful?"

She sat up, arched her back and massaged it. Swiveling her chair around, she faced me. Her expression didn't look promising. "Not really. I found a mention of him in some records relating to Carter High School. Seems he was president of the school's photography club, and won some awards in photo competitions."

No surprises there. The photos I'd seen were definitely taken by someone who knew his way around a camera.

"Anything negative on him?"

She cocked her head and stared at me through narrowed slits. "Is there something I should be looking for?"

"Uh, nothing in particular." I crossed my fingers behind my back. I don't like lying to Heather, even by omission, but like I said, I didn't want to prejudice her research. "Just curious is all."

That seemed to satisfy her. She turned back to her computer. "No, nothing negative. In fact, except for a couple of items about the school photography club, nothing at all. The guy's a real cypher. It's like, except for that one club, he wasn't even at school, or anywhere else for that matter."

Good, she was thorough, and if there was anything, she'd find it. If there was something that raised red flags, I could trust her to recognize it. This way, if she did find something I could trust that it was valid, and not a result of me pushing her in that direction.

"Okay, keep looking. I'm going home."

"Give my best to Sandra," she said, and was back absorbed in her computer search before I'd even turned to the door.

During the drive home, the crush of rush hour traffic kept my mind off the case. Driving in the DC area requires your full attention at all times, but during rush hour, you really have to be on your game. It doesn't matter if it's the morning rush, with people in a hurry to get to some boring office job, or the evening rush as they speed home to catch the late news and a warmed-over TV dinner, the streets are like a slightly less frantic version of demolition derby. People change lanes without signaling, run the red lights, and make turns from the wrong lanes as if their vehicle is the only one on the road. The traffic cameras that had begun appearing all over Montgomery County did force some drivers to lower their speed, so the inevitable rush-hour fender benders resulted in fatalities less often—except when an unwary pedestrian or cyclist was involved, but it didn't lower the number of accidents at all.

I've been lucky, except for one accident shortly after the death of my wife and son, when I'd let myself get distracted waiting for a left turn, a woman had ignored that I had the turn light and rammed into my car as she tried to rush through the intersection. Neither of us were hurt, but it took a tow truck twenty minutes to unentangle our cars. Even so, whenever I had to drive during either morning or evening rush hour, I was pretty wound up by the time I reached my destination.

I pulled up in front of the house next to Sandra's car, turned the engine off, and sat there for a few minutes to let my breathing and pulse to return to normal.

When I was sure I'd my facial muscles were no longer tense, I got out and went inside. She was sitting on the sofa, flipping through the *Washington Post*'s B Section. She looked up at me and smiled.

Damn, I'd forgotten. It was our Friday for eating out.

"Hey, babe," I said. "Give me a few minutes to take a quick shower, and we can go. What're you in the mood for tonight?"

"I sort of have a taste for Chinese," she said. "Maybe, Sichuan. Something spicy would go down well right now."

"Hard day at school, huh?"

She just said, 'hmph,' and ducked her head back behind the paper. Great, she's in a pissy mood about something that happened at school, and I needed to bounce my crazy theory off her. This was beginning to look like it would be an interesting evening. The *gongbao jiding* wouldn't be the only hot thing I'd be dealing with.

Charles Ray

Bad Girls Don't Die

Chapter 22

I took a quick shower, and changed into a pair of gray slacks and a pearl-colored dress shirt. I even wore my best dress shoes.

Her expression wasn't too tense, and she leaned into me when I kissed her left ear. I kept quiet as we walked to the car, though, because she's like me, too much talking when you're chewing on a problem, when the person talking doesn't know what the problem is, doesn't do anything but make it worse.

I remained quiet while I drove, and so did she. In fact, nothing was said until we pulled into the parking lot of the *Sichuan Palace*, a recently opened Chinese restaurant on Rockville Pike, just south of the intersection with Shady Grove Road. The parking lot was almost filled, but there's also a *Domino's Pizza* and a *7-Eleven* in the same tiny shopping mall, and I could see a lot of people entering and leaving both of those establishments. I silently prayed for the restaurant not to be crowded. That would really complicate things. My prayers were answered.

Fewer than half the tables were occupied. The tall, slender Chinese waitress, dressed in a pink *cheongsam* with a slit up the lift side nearly to the top of her thigh, seated us in the front, in a corner that was somewhat separated from the rest of the room by a high bamboo screen. I breathed a sigh of relief. We'd have a bit of privacy, which I sensed we both needed—I knew that I did.

After handing us large plastic-coated menus, she asked us if we'd like anything to drink.

"What Chinese beer do you recommend?" Sandra asked the waitress, smiling for the first time.

"We have *qing dao*," the woman said in heavily accented English. "Very famous Chinese beer. We also have Japan beer, if you like."

"Do you have the large bottles of *qing dao*?" I asked, careful to properly pronounce the 'ch' sound in the first word.

"Yes, big bottle."

I smiled across the table at Sandra. "Bring us two bottles," I said.

"Okay, I bring beer, while you decide what you like to eat."

"Thanks," Sandra said, when she'd scurried off to get our beer. "I knew you'd understand."

"Your day was that rough, was it?"

"You don't know the half of it. And, from the look on your face when you came home, I gather yours was a real circus as well."

I shrugged. "Not so much my day, as a culmination of the whole week. But, look, let's get a sip of beer first, and decide what we want to eat before we spoil the evening with our problems."

At that point, the waitress came back with our beer, two large green bottles of beer and two large tumblers balanced on a big round tray. She set a bottle and tumbler in front of each of us, expertly removed the caps from the bottles, and then, after tucking the tray under her arm, took out her order pad.

"You decide what you want to eat?"

"You up for something really spicy, babe?" I asked Sandra.

"Sure, I'm feeling adventurous tonight."

I looked up at the waitress who waited with her pen poised over her order pad.

"We'll have *gongbao jiding, mapo doufu, congyou bing, bai cai,* and *bai fan,*" I said, smiling as her eyes flared.

"You speak very good Chinese," she said.

"*Bu gan dang.*" I said, reciting the expected 'it's nothing' that a polite Chinese person would respond with after getting a compliment.

Actually, I don't know that much Mandarin, but when I like a country's food, I try to learn the local words for dishes. It gets better service in most places.

"You sure you want so many spicy dish?" she asked.

The *gongbao jiding*, chicken and cashew nuts, and *mapo doufu,* a soup made with soybean curd, are both loaded with red pepper, but tasty. *Congyou bing* are pancakes made with egg and scallions, *bai cai* is white cabbage, and *bai fan* is just plain old boiled white rice. Standard fare for Chinese, especially those from Sichuan Province, even the kids, but the one thing I learned about Asians serving there when I was in the army, is that they are convinced that westerners can't handle their spicier foods. I always had to set them straight.

"Actually, now that you mention it, could you add *huiguo rou* to that. I have a taste for spicy pork." The dish called twice-fried pork, has twice as much pepper as anything except their hot pot dishes, and is great with cold beer.

She looked skeptical, but wrote our order down.

"Food be ready soon," she said, and with an exaggerated swing to her hips, walked away.

"You do that just to mess with people, don't you?" Sandra was smiling wickedly at me.

"Only partly. I also happen to like those particular dishes. It's not my fault that they stereotype their customers. I'll bet she wouldn't have cautioned an Asian who ordered those dishes."

She shrugged and took another swig of her beer. Then she leaned forward with her elbows on the table.

"Okay, which one of us unloads first?" she asked.

I held my glass up in a toast. "Ladies first."

Her expression turned dour.

"We had a horrible case today. One of our ninth graders, a bright little girl, was raped by her older sister's boyfriend."

My beer suddenly tasted sour. "They arrested the son of a bitch, right?"

A single tear formed in the corner of her right eye. "Yes, but not before the sister tried to convince the police that it was consensual sex that just got out of hand."

I almost choked.

"What? You mean this kid's sister sided with her boyfriend against her own blood kin. Holy shit."

"Holy shit is right. If it hadn't been for a nosy neighbor who heard the kid screaming, she might have pulled it off."

"They busted the sister, too, right?"

"I think they wanted to, but the girl said her sister wasn't in the room when the boyfriend attacked her."

"But, you don't believe her?"

She shook her head. "Hell, no. I remember the sister from several years ago when she was at Carter. I think she set the whole thing up, maybe as a joke, and it went wrong. But, Ellen, the victim, worships her older sister, and will not accuse her of anything."

All I could do was shake my head. This, piled atop what I was already wrestling with, was so far beyond my comprehension, we might as well have been discussing events on some alien world. I was raised in an environment where family took care of each other, especially older family members. Even my many years in war zones, with all the inhumanity I'd seen people capable of, that was one constant—people took care of their children as best they could.

Now, this. A woman aiding in the abuse of her younger sister. It was almost too bizarre to be believed. But, I had my own bizarre story.

Her's told, Sandra was now ready to hear mine.

"Okay, that's my shitty day," she said. "What's eating at you?"

The waitress picked that moment to arrive with our food, two small empty plates and two bowls stacked next to larger plates containing our order, which she placed in the center of the table. After a last skeptical look at the two crazy *guei los*, the foreign devils who didn't know what they were doing, she left.

We filled our bowls with rice, and put helpings of everything else on our plates, and plucked wooden chopsticks in red and white paper wrappers from the container in the center of the table. I went first for the twice-fried pork, enjoying the slight burning sensation on my tongue as I chewed it. I followed that with rice, which is the best way to ease the burn until your mouth becomes accustomed to it. Sandra watched me, and copied my movements. The way her cheeks reddened, I knew she felt the peppers, but she smiled and her eyes lit up when the taste kicked in. We were silent as we tried each of our entrees, and then, I put my chopsticks across the rim of my rice bowl, took a sip of beer and began my sorry tale.

She already knew the basics of the case, so I started with my visit to the Birdsong house. As I talked, the look of worry, mixed with a little anger, clouded her face.

"From the looks of it," I said, summing up. "Lena lived in the basement. There's not one sign of her in the rest of the house."

"Do you think he was holding her prisoner there?"

"Oh, she was a prisoner, but not in the way you might think," I said. "After all, he allowed her to attend school, and I think she did some of the shopping."

"Yes, but . . ." Her eyes went wide. "You're not suggesting . . . she was his grandchild, surely he wouldn't—"

"Think about it, babe. She slept in the basement, in that bed. The old man was killed on that bed, and he was nude. I can't see a killer taking his clothes off after killing him."

"It doesn't make any sense. If she were younger, maybe, but she's of legal age now, maybe not in maturity, but by the calendar, she's a woman. I can't imagine her not telling someone."

"Really? What did you just get through telling me about your student and her sister. It's like the Stockholm Syndrome, only worse. When the abuser is a close relative, victims often submit and refuse to rat on them. It doesn't make sense to you or me, but we've never been in that kind of situation."

Her lips trembled. The tears were now in both eyes and threatening to spill onto her cheeks.

"That's horrible. That bastard, may he rot in hell."

"I'm not shedding any tears for him either," I said. "Although, killing him was still illegal. It would have been better to put him in prison, in general population, and let the other cons have him. I hear they really *like* pedophiles in our nation's prisons."

"That poor, tortured girl. Oh, my God. It was probably going on all these years, and she . . . we . . . we failed her. Someone in the school should've suspected something, should've done something."

"What? Other than being reclusive, and shy, what were the signs you should've seen?" She shook her head. "Right. Besides, that's not important right now. What's important is finding her."

"Do you think Joshua Pearl abducted her?"

"Yeah, and so does Buster. He's got every cop in the city, as well as Virginia and Maryland on the lookout for him. I think when we find him we'll find her."

"If she's still alive, that is." She looked like she was about to cry.

"I don't think he'll harm her. I went with Buster today to search his room in the house where he was staying." I told her about the photos. "He's clearly obsessed with her. Probably has been since high school."

"My goodness," she said. "You think he killed the grandfather and took her to protect her?"

"As warped as it sounds, it fits the evidence we've found."

Then, she jerked her head up and looked at me, a shocked expression contorting her face. "You don't think that she might also have been involved in her grandfather's death, do you?"

The thought had crossed my mind, but I'd dismissed it. From all that I'd learned about Lena Birdsong, she was the passive type, who was easily manipulated. It would have taken a long time for Joshua Pearl or anyone else, for that matter, to convince her to do such a horrible thing, despite what her grandfather might've been doing to her. I didn't see Pearl having the opportunity to have that much contact with her, and from the condition of his room, he didn't strike me as the type to conceive of such a plan. Other than his stalking, which was careful and methodical, there were no other signs of that kind of ability. No, this looked to me like a spur of the moment action, something done in a fit of rage and desperation.

"No, frankly, I don't think she has it in her to do something like that," I said.

"Have you shared what you suspect about the grandfather with Buster?"

I shook my head. "No, it didn't seem to be germane to the murder case, and right now, that's his number one priority. He has his sights set on Pearl as the most likely suspect."

She gave me look that I suspect more than a few of her students had been the recipient of, that 'you know better than that' look.

"You should tell him anyway," she said.

Charles Ray

Chapter 23

The next morning, Saturday, at 10:30, sitting on my back porch with bottles of ice cold *Corona* in our hands, I did just that.

He looked angry, but not at all surprised.

"I should be pissed at you for not tellin' me right away, bro," he said. "But, I kept something from you, so we're even."

Not sure that he wasn't jerking me around, I glared at him. "It wasn't something that might've helped me find Lena, was it?"

He smiled that wolfish smile of his, and I knew he'd just been yanking my chain a little.

"Naw, you know I wouldn't do a thing like that." He took a long pull of *Corona*, and then wiped his mouth with the back of his hand. "It was the results of the lab examination of the crime scene."

"Oh, yeah, you're right. I doubt that would help me figure out where she is."

A strange expression flitted across his face.

"But, it might help you figure out whether she left willingly or not."

"Huh?"

"The lab guys took the sheet and . . . some of the other bed clothes in for a more detailed analysis." He seemed to be struggling with what he wanted to say. "They found some . . . unusual traces on the sheet. Mixed in with the blood, were traces of . . . semen."

Shit. That didn't surprise me. Unfortunately, it was validating my gut.

"The semen, of course, was from the victim?"

"Yeah."

"Any chance he might have spurted as he died?" I asked. "You know, like the bladder and bowels loosen, maybe that function does to."

He looked shocked. Imagine, Buster Mayweather shocked at anything. I know, it's a hard picture to form in your brain.

"Hell," he said, after gulping. "I don't know. But, that's not the point anyway. According to the techs, the stains weren't all made at the same time. Some of 'em, in fact, were pretty old."

The human mind's a funny thing. It tries its best to reorder even facts to make them comfortable for us to endure. Unlike the gut which just reacts to the world that is, the gray matter between our ears is always trying to remake things.

"So, the old guy was jerking off in the basement, so what. What does that have to do with the girl being gone? Oh, you mean, maybe she caught him doing it, got grossed out, and ran away?"

He gave me one of the looks Sandra gives me when I say something stupid. On her it's intimidating, on him it's downright scary.

"C'mon, bro," he said. "You told me yourself, the girl slept in the basement. In fact, that it looks like she spent most of her time down there."

He was being incredibly patient with me, leading me carefully, step-by-step back to my own conclusion.

"Yeah, it did look that way."

Then, he zigged when I thought he was about to zag.

"The ME says the victim had sex shortly before he died," he said.

"No," I said. "Are they sure?"

"Pretty damn close to a hundred percent sure. You know what that means?"

I swallowed the bile that was rising in my throat. "I know, but I don't want to say it. Hell, I don't even want to think about it."

Now, his face was contorted in fury.

"Well, bro, let me say it for the both of us," he said. "You got it right. That dirt bag was abusing his granddaughter. You wonder why I didn't seem surprised when you told me? It's because the ME and the lab techs already told me. And, the fucking bad part is, he probably been doin' it for years."

Now that it was on the table, it was no less unpleasant to think about, but at least it wasn't so hard to talk about.

"You think maybe Joshua Pearl knew about it?" I asked.

"You saw them damn photos. That kid was on that girl like flies on rotten meat. Bet you even money he knew. And, I think he just snapped."

"Shit," I said. "You got two kids with fragile emotional states and a shitload of trauma out there somewhere. That's a pretty explosive combination. We've got to find them."

"Tell me about it. You know, when we find this kid, I don't know whether to shoot him or thank him for ridding the world of a monster."

"You won't do either, my friend."

"Oh yeah, how do you know. What am I gonna do, then?"

"You're going to slap the cuffs on him, and read him his rights."

Charles Ray

Chapter 24

The rest of the weekend was uneventful. No new leads, no breaking events, just Sandra and me, sitting on the porch, taking advantage of the amazingly mild weather, and enjoying each other's company.

Monday, after getting up early and doing a nice run through the forest, followed by a vigorous workout on the heavy bag in the gym, we showered together, horsed around a little, ate a hearty breakfast, and wished each other a great day. She went off to school, and I drove to the office, in such a good mood that, for once, I wasn't even bothered by the mindlessness of the morning rush-hour drivers.

Heather is not bothered by rush hour traffic. I'm convinced that's because she gets to the office long before rush hour starts, and never leaves in the evening until it's over and done with. She is almost always at her desk when I arrive, looking calm and together, sipping her fragrant tea and idly gazing at her computer screen. Occasionally, she'll put her tea cup down and make a note on a steno pad she keeps handy, and most of the time, she'll be humming some unknown tune quietly. She looked so serene, I hated to disturb her.

But, we had a case to solve.

"Hey, Honey Bunch," I said, using a nickname I'd tagged her with when we first met, and one that she only allowed me to use, and then, only in private. "Anything new on our case?"

"As a matter of fact, boss man," she said, hitting back with her tag for me, back when I was her boss and not her partner. "I just might have something. That remains to be seen. Want to grab your second cup of coffee and have a seat?"

I did, and I did.

Coffee in hand, straddling the visitor's chair at the side of her desk, I gave her my best alert stare.

"Okay, I'm ready. Shoot."

She flipped pages on the steno pad until she was at the beginning. From the look on her face, I settled in for a long explanation. Like a lot of computer geeks, Heather is proud of her ability to ferret out information from the Internet, and, also like geeks, she has difficulty just getting to the point; she has to show you the steps she took to get there.

"I was having no luck at all searching for information about Joshua Pearl under his name," she said, and flipped a page. "Then, I thought it might help if I went about it indirectly. You know, instead of searching for *him*, I'd find someone who might know or be connected to him, and see if their records refer to him in any way.

More page flipping.

"Then, it occurred to me, he had to have parents at some point in time, so I called Sandra at Carter, since he went there, and asked for his parents' names. Even though they'd died by the time he got to high school, they were still listed on his records as his parents— don't you just love bureaucracies and their forms?— so, with the names, Elwood and Katherine Pearl, in hand I started a whole new search. Would you like to guess what I found?"

I took a sip of coffee and gave her the evil eye.

"You know I wouldn't. I wouldn't even know where to start."

She made a face. "You're no fun, you know. You could at least humor me once or twice. Oh, never mind. I forgot, you have no sense of humor. Anyway, his parents weren't on social media. No surprise there. They were dead before social media became the thing. But, like most Americans, they had drivers' licenses, paid taxes, and owned property, and all those records, or most of them, have been computerized in the state of Maryland."

As she spoke, I had one of those 'eureka' moments. Property records. He lived somewhere before he became an orphan, and a scared animal will always try to make its way back to the nest.

"You know where they were living when they died?"

"I do, it's in Takoma Park, not the District, but Montgomery County, in one of the poorer neighborhoods that hasn't yet been gentrified."

"I imagine someone else's living there now, but at least it gives me a place to start looking for him."

Her face lit up with a big smile.

"Oh, you're going to love this part," she said. "I can't find a record of the house changing ownership. As far as Maryland's concerned, it still belongs to the Pearl family."

"You mean it's been vacant all these years?"

"If by vacant, you mean a family that mows the lawn and keeps it neat, yes. But, if you mean vacant as in the taxes are unpaid, or no one's been using it as a crash pad, the answer is no to the first, and I doubt it to the second."

"Whoa, you mean someone's been keeping the taxes current?"

"Didn't I just say that? It's not a big deal. Despite Montgomery County's high taxes, the annual bill on the Pearl place is really quite low. Like I said, it's in a poor neighborhood that hasn't really kept pace economically with the rest of the county."

I'll be double-dog damned. That sly little devil had probably been using whatever money he could scrape together to pay the taxes, giving him the perfect bolt hole when he needed to hide out, and a little voice in my mind was telling me that that's exactly where I'd find him. I leaned forward and kissed Heather's smooth forehead.

"You, Honey Bunch, are worth every penny I pay you. You just might've solved two cases."

"Two? I thought you were just looking for the Birdsong girl." She's cute when she looks puzzled.

I told her what Buster and I had concluded from the evidence we'd collected so far. Her puzzlement turned first to shock, and then to anger.

"You, you mean you think that old man was . . . abusing that poor girl, and you think Joshua Pearl killed the old geezer to rescue her? Oh, my."

That's Heather for you. Most people would've said, 'what the fuck,' or if they wanted to be semi-polite, 'holy shit,' but my Heather rarely used such words, not even after working with me and seeing some real mean crap for more than a decade.

"I was pretty sure the old man was abusing her after I examined the house for myself, but the information Buster gave me clinched it. As for Pearl killing the old man, the evidence points to that, and Buster's pretty convinced."

"You've got that look in your eye and you're using the tone of voice that says you're not so sure about that part."

I was, and for the life of me I couldn't figure out why. Something just didn't click. Sure, the Pearl kid was a stalker, an addict, and a loner with a little hideout that even his foster mother knew nothing about. But, I hadn't seen anything that made me think he was a killer, especially someone who could slit a man's throat the way old man Birdsong's throat had been cut. I'd gotten a glimpse of it before they bagged the body and hauled it away. Whoever did that had made one forceful swipe that opened his throat from his left ear and right across his windpipe. There wasn't a sign of the slightest hesitation, which usually happens the first time someone uses a knife on a living creature, especially another human. The killer was either incredibly experienced and callous, or completely enraged to the point that there was no thought behind the act, just an explosive lashing out.

Of course, solving Birdsong's murder wasn't my problem. Buster had that one, and if he could make a case, I'd congratulate him on the good work.

So, why was my mind at that moment more focused on who killed the old man than on finding his missing granddaughter?

I stood and shoved back from the chair, but she held her hand up in a 'wait a moment' gesture. "There was one other thing I found," she said. "It won't help your case, but it was interesting, so I made a note of it."

"You never know what'll be helpful, kiddo. What was it?"

"It was a Myspace posting by one of the Carter High cheerleaders. Seems that Joshua decided not to be a hermit for once, and attended the football rally during his junior year. When some of the kids started picking on him, the school's star running back, a kid named Bill Banning, came to his rescue. You should've seen the comments. They were calling him 'Banning's Bitch,' and a few other choice nicknames. I'll bet that's the last school activity he participated in."

"A jock stood up for a geek? That's something you don't see every day."

"Apparently, Banning was the only white kid on the football team, and was something of a hunk. Maybe he just didn't like seeing this puny little kid being harassed by his teammates."

"Did he get called any names?"

"I said he was a hunk, *and* a star football player. What do you think?"

"Joshua the Geek took all the heat."

She pointed her forefinger at me and made a clucking sound with her tongue.

"You are one smart cookie, boss man."

Chapter 25

As soon as Heather's data dump was done, I went into my office and called Buster. I used the phone on my desk, but called his cell.

"Whatcha got, pal?" he asked. He was getting to be a real expert with mobile phones. Now, he had my office phone ID on it.

"I think I know where you can find Joshua Pearl," I said.

"Well, don't make me wait all day. Where is he?"

I gave him the address.

"Shit," he said. "I'll have to call the Montgomery County cops in for this one. I'd invite you to come along, but I'm not sure they'll go along with a civilian in the middle of what could be a hairy takedown."

I hadn't expected to be invited. I don't really know any of the cops in Montgomery County, at least I haven't worked with any of them in a while, so it's hardly likely they'd be as willing as Buster is sometimes to ignore departmental regulations on my behalf. It was going to be enough problems for him to get them to agree to him going along on the bust, and they'd probably do it only because it was a District case. Besides, I had other plans.

"No problem, amigo," I said. I tried to put a little disappointment in my voice. No sense alerting him to what I was planning.

"No sweat, bro. I'll fill you in as soon as it goes down."

I thanked him and hung up. I had a lot to do, and not a whole lot of time to do it.

The first thing I did was tell Heather that I needed to go home for something, and might be out for several hours. The next was sprint down to the parking lot, hop into my car, and violate several local speed limits getting home.

Knowing how bureaucracies work, I figured it would take Buster three or four hours to coordinate a raid on Pearl's place by the Montgomery County police, maybe even a bit longer if there was pushback at the idea of him going along. That should give me the time I needed to do what I had planned to do.

If Pearl was there, and if he had Lena, my intent was to rescue her, and leave him to the cops—provided he didn't resist too much, in which case, I'd still leave him to the cops, but he would be in no shape to resist arrest. That would piss Buster off, but not nearly as much as it'd piss off the local cops, but I was willing to take the heat.

I parked in front of the house and went inside. In the bedroom, I changed into black cargo pants and a black long sleeve shirt. I strapped my K-Bar knife to my ankle, and as an extra precaution slipped a sap I'd gotten from Blood Raine into one of the pants pockets. I was taking a chance that Pearl wouldn't have a gun, thinking that if he did have one he would've used it on Gabriel Birdsong. My final piece of equipment was a pair of plastic disposable kitchen gloves from the counter near the sink, just in case I had to handle anything.

Satisfied that I was as prepared as I could be, I went outside, fired the Bug up, and headed for Takoma Park.

I made good time from my house, driving on River Road until I hit Wisconsin Avenue, where I turned north and drove until I got to East-West Highway. That took me almost to Takoma Park, where I used side streets until I was on the narrow, barely-two-lane street where Joshua Pearl had spent his childhood.

The area was definitely low-rent. A collection of one- and two-story houses with precariously leaning fences and poorly maintained yards. I saw few people, either in the yards or on the streets, which didn't surprise me. This was one of the working-class neighborhoods populated mainly by Latin American immigrants, many of them fleeing violence and turmoil in their home countries. The adults would all be out working at minimum-wage jobs and the kids would be in schools, or street gangs. The few too old to work and too young for school would probably be inside, their eyes glued to one of the many Spanish-language TV stations in the area.

I drove past the address Heather had found, happy not to see black vans with tinted windows and SWAT logos on the sides. Buster and his friends hadn't arrived yet. I parked a block east of the house, got out and locked the car doors.

I walked back toward the house, ducking between two houses at the first opportunity, and made my way along the unpaved service road that ran between the houses on this street and the next street over. In the distance, I could hear a dog barking, but it seemed to be beyond my destination.

The Pearl house didn't have a fence. The backyard was a square of packed dirt with two or three clumps of limp, yellow grass. The house was quiet, but then, so were the houses on either side. I made my way cautiously to the back door.

The window in the door was so smeared with grime I couldn't see inside, so I flattened myself against the wall and peeked into the window beside the door. I could only see a portion of the kitchen, but it looked like no one had prepared a meal in it for a long time. The refrigerator door was open, and there was no light coming from inside. A broken glass sat on the sink next to the basin. It looked as grimy as the window in the door. If Pearl was using this place, he must be subsisting on takeout food, because anyone eating food prepared in the cesspool I was looking at was flirting with a bad case of food poison.

More importantly, though, I didn't see any movement, nor did I hear any sounds other than the normal creaking of wooden buildings. No humming air conditioner, no background buzz of electricity flowing through wires, and no knocking of water pipes.

I tried the door knob. It was locked, but the door vibrated as I tried turning the knob. Over time, the door had warped and was loose in the frame. I grabbed hold of the knob and pushed toward the hinges and inward at the same time. There was a loud screeching sound and the door swung inward. The rusty hasp was still hanging from the tongue of the lock.

I quickly stepped inside and eased the door shut. Standing still for a few minutes, I listened to see if the noise of my entry had alerted anyone. I heard nothing.

I crossed the kitchen and entered what had once been the dining room. Nothing was left but a scarred and warped dining table and three chairs, one of which only had three legs, and was balanced against the table. Some crumpled pieces of paper lay at one end of the table. I made a mental note to check them after I'd checked the place out.

With the Buster and the county police likely to arrive at any moment, there was no time for a methodical search, so I quickly walked through the rooms downstairs, finding nothing except signs in the living room that someone had sat on the ratty sofa and ate pizza within the past month or so—the moldy box was on the coffee table—and small, crumpled plasticine envelopes still had residue of some powdery substance in them at the side of the sofa. I assumed the substance was cocaine, only because that just happened the drug of choice for the suburbs, but it could also have been heroin. The important thing, though, was that there was no one at home. Same for the upstairs, two bedrooms and a shared bath. I saved the basement for last, but could just as well have knocked it off in a few seconds when I did the downstairs. It was just a cobweb=festooned space, probably half the footprint of the house above, lit by two hanging bulbs when I flipped the switch at the top of the stairs, it contained, in addition to the aforementioned cobwebs, a few dust-covered boxes and pieces of furniture. I looked down at the stairs. The layer of dust coating them was undisturbed.

I turned and went back to the dining room and the pieces of paper. I pulled the plastic gloves from my pocket, slipped them on, and picked up the first piece of paper. I carefully smoothed the slip of paper out, noting that it was a cash register receipt, but it was so faded I couldn't make out what had been purchased. I did note dark marks that seemed to bleed through, so I turned it over. On the back, written with a black marker, was, **25-WB-x**. I turned it back over, pushed it aside, and picked up another, which was a ticket stub for the movie theater in downtown Rockville, across the street from the Rockville Metro station. On a hunch, I turned it over. Again, a black marker had been used, and **10-WB-no** was written in the same crabby hand that had done the note on the back of the receipt.

There were six more pieces of paper, cash register receipts for the most part, but also what looked like part of a page torn from a small flip pad, and each had a number, the initials, **WB**, and two-digit numbers. All but two of them had **no** following the letters; the two exceptions had an **x** at the end.

It was an intriguing puzzle, but didn't give me a clue as to where Pearl or Lena might be. A quick glance at my watch showed me that I was pushing the envelope on time. Buster and his entourage were surely on the way, if not already in the neighborhood, and I didn't want to have to explain why I was there.

I placed the papers back on the table in a haphazard pile, made my way through the kitchen and out the door, pulling it as close to shut as I could manage given its condition. I only hoped that in their search of the place, which wasn't likely to turn up anything, the damage to the door would be lost in the general decrepitude of the place.

Walking quickly, but carefully, I made my way down the service road until I was just about where I'd left my car.

I had it in gear and was just pulling away from the curb when I looked in the rearview mirror and saw the first black van pull up a few houses from Pearl's place. Almost immediately, black-clad officers with face shields and assault weapons started pouring from the back and lining up on the sidewalk. A car pulled in behind the van, and I saw Buster, wearing an armored vest, step put and start toward the officers. Hoping he wouldn't spot my car, I made a quick left turn at the first intersection I came to, and stepped on the gas to get as far away from there as possible.

Charles Ray

Chapter 26

I was just entering the office when the phone rang. Heather picked it up, identified herself, and listened as a muffled voice on the other end said something I couldn't make out. I was just passing her desk, when she held up a finger. She put a hand over the mouthpiece.

"It's Buster," she said. "He said he needs to talk to you."

I kept moving toward my office. "Put him through."

The light on my phone was blinking. I picked it up.

"Hey, Buster, how'd the bust go?" I tried to sound completely at ease, as if I'd been doing nothing but sitting behind my desk waiting for his call.

"The bust was mostly a bust," he said. "There was no one home. We did find some stuff, though, that indicates this Pearl dude was dealing coke."

So, the white powder residue was coke. "How'd you find that out?" I asked.

"We found some plastic envelopes with a little powder residue. It still has to be tested by the county lab, but I smelled it, and it was cocaine."

"Maybe he was using. What indicated that he was selling the stuff?"

I could hear the sound of papers being shuffled. Even Buster, a street cop down to the soles of his size-twelve feet, had to do it.

"We found a stash under the first step leadin' down to the basement. They were taped to the underside with duct tape," he said. "The envelopes were the same as the ones lying around upstairs. Looks like he was not only dealing, but was samplin' his own goods.

Damn, if I'd had more time, I might have found that myself. The basement looked like it hadn't been used lately, and I'd never thought to look under the stairs. The county cops were a lot more proficient than I would have thought, or at least, more thorough.

"I'd never have figured Pearl for a dealer," I said. "His foster mother said he was using something, but other than stalking the Birdsong girl, I didn't see anything in what we found on him to indicate he'd be doing something as enterprising as dealing the stuff."

I knew as soon as I said it that I *had* seen indications, but I hadn't connected the dots. That was obviously how he'd acquired the money to keep up the taxes on his family's house. I mentally kicked myself. But, Buster wasn't finished.

"The thing is," he said. "The county cops don't think he was a big-time dealer. They've been seein' more coke in Rockville and Gaithersburg, a hell of a lot more than he could've been supplyin', and he'd never come up on their radar, so it ain't likely he was sellin' the stuff out there."

"So, he has a supplier, or a boss."

"That's the theory they're workin' on, and I think they're right. 'Course, that don't do shit to help me nail the little fucker for killin' Birdsong. He's in the wind, and I don't have a clue where he might be."

Then, a thought hit me right between the eyes.

"If he has a dealer, it's more than likely someone he trusts. If he wasn't at his old house, I'll bet you two dinners at Mom's that he's holed up with that person. Find him, and you'll find Pearl." I didn't add, and most likely find Lena Birdsong as well.

"Shit, you're right. We hadn't thought of that. I'll call the county guys and pass that along. Any luck in gettin' a line on the missing girl?"

"No, but I think when you guys find Pearl, she'll be with him."

"You don't think she might just have gotten tired of the old man . . . pawin' her, and she took off?"

"No, I can't buy that theory, Buster," I said. "If she ran away, where's Pearl's motive to kill the old man? You said yourself that you think he did it to save her from the abuse."

"Yeah, I did say that, didn't I? For what it's worth, I think you're right, but you can't rule out her just runnin' away."

No, I couldn't, not really. But, it didn't make any sense. She had no credit cards, no bank account—according to Heather's research—and, if she was going to run away, the time to do it would've been a few years earlier, not at her age, and not without the resources to survive on her own. Maybe a tiny part of my brain thought it possible that she'd run away, but the big lobes knew better. No, wherever Joshua Pearl was, Lena Birdsong was with him. The big question, though; would we find them in time?

"Well," I said. "Keep me posted . . . if you can."

"Will do, bro. Lemme know the next time you want to go to Mom's."

I cut the connection without telling him about the numbers and initials on the papers on the dining table. I was pretty sure they'd found them, and they were now probably in an evidence bag at the county police offices. I doubted they'd made any more of them than I had, or else Buster would've said something. Maybe they didn't realize the significance of them; I know I didn't when I first saw them, but while talking to Buster, they began to make sense. If Pearl was dealing drugs, those initials either indicated a customer or they were the initials of his dealer. Given the amounts, most likely grams of coke, and the fact that the initials were on all the pieces of paper, I was pretty sure 'WB' was Pearl's dealer. Now, I just had to find him before the cops did. If this guy was a big-time dope dealer, there was a good chance he was sitting on an armory, and wouldn't go down without a fight. If that happened, the chances of Lena Birdsong becoming collateral damage, to use the euphemistic phrase the military had coined to describe innocent civilian deaths, were pretty good, or pretty bad, depending upon how you chose to look at things.

It was time to set Heather's search mode to hyperspeed, or whatever the correct computer term was.

Chapter 27

She was taking a break when I walked out of my office, leaning back in her chair with her ever-present of tea that smelled like a flower shop, with a look of pure bliss on her elfin face.

The blissful look turned to her all-business look when she saw me looming over her desk. Setting her tea cup on the desk near her keyboard, she swiveled her chair around and looked up at me.

"Don't tell me," she said. "You just had a brilliant idea, and you want me to drop everything and find the facts to support it."

Sometimes it's like she can read my mind. I wasn't, however, going down without at least one shot back.

"If I don't tell you, how will you know what to do?" I kept my face as placid and innocent-looking as possible.

She blinked. She looked down, looked back up at me, and blinked again. Then, understanding dawned in her baby blues—I'd one-upped her in the quips department. Oh, hallelujah! She smiled. Heather's a gracious loser.

"Okay, point yours," she said. "What do you want me to do?"

I explained the cryptic notes I'd found in Joshua Pearl's vacant house. "I think Pearl is probably with his drug supplier, hiding out, but the police have no idea who he is," I said, summing up. "I think, though, the mysterious 'MB" might be him."

She'd been making notes in a steno pad that mysteriously appeared while I was talking. She paused, her pen hovering above the surface of the paper, and looked up at me.

"You're probably right, but I wonder what those numbers represent?"

"Probably quantities of drugs would be my guess."

She cocked her head to the side. "And, the 'x' and '?', what do they mean?"

"Probably nothing important," I said, shorthand for, I hadn't the faintest idea, and was hoping she'd find out and tell me.

She propped her steno book up next to her laptop and hit a key bringing the screen to life.

"Okay, then. Go back to your office, and do whatever it is you do in there, and let me work. I'll buzz you, or come in when I find something."

I liked the way she talked, and the self-assured gleam in her eyes. She was like a bloodhound that's been given a strong scent to follow. There was no *if* she found anything, she was pretty damn sure she *would* find something.

Feelings of confidence, and eager anticipation warmed me as I went back into my inner sanctum and closed the door.

Those feelings didn't last too long, though. Within fifteen minutes of sitting behind my desk, impatience came calling, and settled in for a long stay. Because of his presence, frustration was not far behind. A watched pot doesn't boil any faster for being watched, but Heather definitely does slow down when you're peeking over her shoulder or interrupting her every few minutes asking, 'have you found anything yet,' so I swallowed my impatience and frustration and turned my own computer on.

It took a few minutes for it to boot up—a term I never understood, since it hadn't anything on it resembling a boot, or even a slipper—then a few minutes were killed deleting all the junk email that clogged up my inbox every day. That job done, I fired up the installed chess game, a total time waster considering I only won against the computer once in every twenty or twenty-five games, but preferable to sitting gazing out the window at the wispy clouds or the gleaming condos.

I was about four moves from losing my tenth game when my office door swung inward, and Heather marched through.

She took a seat in my guest-client chair and put her steno pad on her crossed knees.

I turned the computer off mid-game and gave her my full attention, knowing from her expression that I was in for a long explanation.

"First, I have to tell you, I haven't identified Joshua Pearl's drug supplier," she said. "But, I have found out more about him, and that might be helpful in figuring out where he might be holed up."

I nodded. "That's the most important thing. Finding his dealer is the cops' concern, not mine, unless it tells us where he is—or, more accurately, where Lena is."

"Quite by accident I ran across this paper written by a former teacher at Carter High School, who left to pursue her doctorate. It was about socially awkward teens and their societal coping problems." She peered down at her pad. "I started reading it mostly out of curiosity, but then I came to a description of an unnamed student, and realized that it seemed like our boy. What she had to say about his personality and social maladjustment squared with the other stuff we've learned."

"Yeah, we already know the guy's a geek who doesn't make friends easily, but how does this help us find him?"

"Just that," she said, pouting at me. "He doesn't make friends easily, and wouldn't trust a stranger."

I held up a finger, a glimmer of understanding beginning to flicker in my mind.

"So, he wouldn't get involved in something like drug dealing with just anyone, it would have to be someone he knew and trusted."

"Exactly, and since he didn't have all that many friends, we just need to talk to the teachers at Carter who were there at the same time he was, and make a list. It couldn't be all that long."

We could do that, but that glimmer of inspiration was getting brighter, and I didn't think we'd have to.

"That might not be necessary," I said. "We need to find one person, and I think I just might know who that is."

"You do? Who?" The look she gave me was priceless. I might've been a talking dog.

"Remember that social media post you showed me? The one where one of the jocks came to his rescue? What was that kid's name?"

She closed her eyes tight in concentration. "Uh, Bill something—"

"Bill Banner," I said. "And, what is Bill short for?"

"William. Oh my, William Banner . . . 'WB'. You think this former high school athlete is Joshua Pearl's drug supplier?"

"I'd be willing to stake my reputation on it. I don't believe in coincidences, and you have to admit, given Pearl's personality, and the congruence of the initials, it makes perfect sense."

She thought about it for a few seconds, and then began bobbing her head up and down.

"You're right. Many high school jocks, once the glory days of high school are over, end up pumping gas or mopping up messes in supermarkets. If this kid didn't make it into college on a scholarship, I can see him turning to drug dealing."

"And, what better way to stay below the radar than having one of your old geek buddies doing the transactions on the street for you. Heather, find William Banner, and I think we'll have found Pearl and Lena."

The bloodhound-on-the-scent look was back in her eyes. "I'm on it."

I might as well have been the invisible man at that point. She was totally absorbed in by her computer screen as her fingers flew over the keys.

Feeling totally unnecessary, I returned to my office, sat behind my desk, leaned back and stared at the ceiling. I didn't feel like letting the computer kick my butt at chess, so I did the next best thing, I did nothing.

Well, not exactly nothing, because even when I'm meditating my mind is working. I was mentally reviewing the case, trying to fit the new piece into the puzzle. Were we right about William Banner, was he the mysterious 'WB' on the slips of paper in Pearl's living room? And, if that was so, what was his role in Lena Birdsong's disappearance?

A lot of questions with no answers. No answers, that is, until Heather rapped on my door and opened it.

"I got a possible address for William Banner," she said.

Chapter 28

The dust tickling her nose woke her up. She was instantly aware of where she was, but something about her surroundings confused her. For one thing, even though she hadn't been awakened, she sensed that there was more than one other person in the room with her while she slept. She didn't know how she knew, but the thought was a burning certainty.

She was also uncomfortable. In addition to the dust that seemed to increase with each breath, she was beginning to get tired of her own sweaty odor; her mouth tasted foul from not being able to brush her teeth; and she was beginning to get that tickling sensation in her crotch that signaled the beginning of her period. She wondered if her captors had thought to lay in a supply of sanitary napkins. If not, the basement was going to get quite ripe very quickly, because ever since her first one, she'd had heavy flows that, frankly, reeked, smelled so bad, in fact, that in high school she just stayed home during her periods to avoid the stinky-eye looks and snide behind-the-back comments from the other girls whenever she went to the locker room.

Then, there was one other thing. She hadn't noticed it at first, but as she settled into being awake, and still being unable to see the far wall of the space in which she was confined, her other senses seemed to have heightened. Her sense of smell, of course, which she wished hadn't, because she was betting tired of smelling herself, and her sense of hearing. That latter one had been a little bit frightening at first. The sound of rats scurrying about, for instance, sent shivers through her body, and had her wondering when they would develop the courage to come closer to explore what could very well be a new source of food.

Despite not knowing how long she'd been a prisoner in this dusty dungeon, she was beginning to come to know her environment. The rustling and chirping of the rats in their far corner no longer bothered her as much as they did at first. In fact, it had begun to be a source of comfort. At least, she knew she wasn't alone. She now knew every sound of this dusty, dark—well, actually, semi-dark, place. The thumping of the pipes was a counterpoint to the rustling of the rats, and the creaking of settling timbers were the lullaby that sang her to her fitful periods of sleep, which she tried as hard as she could to avoid, in an effort to keep the troubling dreams at bay.

Then, there was a new sound, one she hadn't heard before. The pipes thumped louder, and the thumping was accompanied by a rushing noise, which she soon recognized as water pushing through corroded pipes. Someone had flushed a toilet. There was someone else in the house. She focused all her being on that sound, and was soon rewarded with the sound of something scraping against the floor above her head, which was followed by the soft thump of shoes.

She listened carefully. Someone was moving around above her, and it didn't sound like they were trying to conceal their presence.

It must be him. The son of a bitch who chained me up here. Her first instinct was to scream or shout to get his attention, but something held her back. Was it fear or curiosity that kept her silent? She wasn't sure, but she remained silent and still, not moving so much as a finger. Would whoever it was come down? A part of her wanted him to, but another feared what might happen if he came down and found her awake and aware.

She heard muffled sounds. Voices? She couldn't tell, but they seemed to be rising and falling, or was it more than one person? Was she in the clutches of some cult or gang? What did they have in mind for her?

The voices—for she had now decided that's what they were—ceased. There was more scraping, followed by a sharp crack like a car backfiring. And, then, there was silence. The silence spooked her even more than the noises.

Suddenly, a shaft of orange light appeared to her left. Slowly, she turned her head, and saw the outline of wooden steps leading up, vague and indistinct at the bottom, but in sharper outline as they soared upwards. She wasn't in a position to see the door, but she knew the door to the basement had been opened. A dark shadow appeared, draping itself over the wooden steps. It grew larger, and she could hear steps on the stairs, and they creaked as weight was placed upon them.

The shadow was followed by a darker shape, which, as it reached the bottom of the stairs, resolved itself into a roughly humanoid form, but with the light behind it, she couldn't make out any features.

The dark shape moved forward, still in shadow, and then almost merging with the darkness of the basement as it stepped out of the orange rectangle of light from the door. It stopped about ten feet from her, going as still as a statue. She could hear the raspy sound of breathing.

She could remain silent no longer. "Who are you? W-why are you k-keeping me prisoner here?"

"Hello, Lena," a slightly familiar voice said. "It's nice to see you again. You've become a beautiful woman."

"Who are you?" It came out almost as a cry.

"You don't remember me? Doesn't matter, I remember you. You're mine now."

"W-what are you going to do?"

The shadow didn't move. The voice, when it came, was disembodied, as if it came from some concealed speaker.

"You'll find out, little darling. You and I are gonna have us a lot of fun."

The dark form started moving toward her. At first, she squeezed her eyes shut. She wanted to cry, but knew somehow that crying would do her no good.

"D-don't touch me," she said with as much force as she could muster. "Let me go."

"Oh, baby, I can't do that. I've been waitin' for this too long. You're mine now."

Then, the form was close enough for her to barely make out human features. She stared at the face looming over her. Recognition came slowly, but when it did, she screamed.

Chapter 29

The only known address she could find for William Banner was just off Viers Mill Road north of Randolph Road in Rockville. I wasn't familiar with the area except from occasionally driving Viers Mill Road on the way somewhere else. My recollection was of modest, middle- and working-class residences, and a large Latin immigrant presence along a good part of that stretch of the street that connected Rockville Pike in Rockville with Georgia Avenue in Silver Spring. I wondered if Banner had relocated there after high school, or even if it was the same William Banner who'd attended Carter High School in the District, but Heather assured me that his profile matched, and she was pretty confident that he was the same person.

Before paying him a visit, I went home to prepare myself. I debated calling Buster, but with nothing more to go on, and after one of my tips had already resulted in no arrest—the county cops weren't thrilled to know they'd missed a drug dealer—I didn't want to put him through it again until I had something solid.

This called for stealth; a night operation, after the streets were quiet and all the honest people, except those working night shifts, were at home safely tucked in bed.

After getting home, I put on my night operation gear; black pants, black shirt, and a balaclava to cover my face and head to prevent glints off smooth skin giving my position away. K-Bar knife was strapped to my ankle, and the sap was in my pocket. Just in case I encountered any evidence Buster might need for his case, I put a pair of plastic gloves in the pocket of my cargo pants. I put my night vision goggles on the coffee table. I went into the kitchen, made a pot of coffee and a peanut butter and ham sandwich, which I took back to the living room. I'd finished the sandwich, and was on my second cup of coffee when Sandra got home from school.

Her eyes narrowed when she saw how I was dressed, but other than that, she showed nothing. She kissed me on top of the head as she passed on her way to the bedroom. I could feel the tension in her body.

A few minutes later, dressed in mid-thigh-length shorts and a plain white tee shirt, with a glass of white wine in her hand, she was back.

"Where to this time?" she asked.

I told her.

Her brow wrinkled. "This William Banner is a drug dealer?"

"Yeah," I said. "We think so."

"And, you're going into his house unarmed?"

"I have my K-Bar and a really good billy club."

"I read somewhere that drug dealers are almost always armed to the teeth, with automatic weapons," she said. "How will a knife or a club fare against an automatic rifle?"

"In order to shoot me, he has to see me." I ran my hand from my shoulder to my waist. "I'm going in well after dark."

She shrugged and plopped down onto my lap, and threw her arms around my neck.

"Why do I even bother trying to talk you out of these foolish forays of yours?" She nuzzled my neck.

"Because you love me, and you worry about me," I said.

"There is that, and you're pretty nice to have around. When are you going?"

I looked at my watch. It was 6:15. With an estimated twenty-five-minute drive, if I planned to breach Banner's perimeter at midnight, I had over five hours.

"I thought I'd leave around 11:00," I said. "I ate a sandwich, but I have time to fix you something."

"I'll fix a sandwich later," she said. "Right now, I have something else in mind."

Two hours later, I had to shower and get dressed all over again, and she had to prepare a very late supper, but it was worth it.

After that, we sat shoulder to shoulder on the couch while she ate her sandwich and salad and drank a glass of white wine. I had another cup of coffee.

At 11:00 on the dot, I kissed her goodnight, told her not to wait up for me, and took off for Rockville.

Getting into Rockville from my place is easy, more so late at night when there's hardly any traffic on River Road. I took a left onto Falls Road in the center of Potomac Village, and about five minutes quicker than I'd estimated, was on Viers Mill Road and nearing my turn onto the street where one Mr. William Banner held court.

Charles Ray

The street, two lanes with parking on both sides turning it into just over one lane, was dark and quiet. The number of old junkers, vans, pickups, and stake trucks ensured that no one would pay much attention to my Volkswagen, just another old car among a bunch of old cars. I parked a block from the address, and sat there a while to make sure there was no one walking along who might give an alarm and let whoever might be inside the house know I was around.

When I was satisfied that no late-night revelers were out and about, I eased the door open and slid out of the car. I closed the door gently to minimize the noise, checked my gear, and started making my way toward the house.

About halfway there, I heard a familiar 'crack,' the sound of a small caliber weapon. I couldn't be sure, but it sounded like it came from the house, which was a dark shape against the trees and sky. I couldn't see any lights inside, but did see a dark van parked in the driveway. My gut told me there was someone inside, probably with the curtains closed. No surprise there. If Pearl and Banner were dealing, they wouldn't want some passerby to see them at work. It made it difficult to get a fix on who was inside, or if they were armed, but had the advantage of them also not being able to see me approaching.

One house before my target destination, I went between two houses to the service road and made my way to the address. Like Pearl's place, the backyard wasn't fenced in, but it was littered with empty beer bottles and crumpled and greasy pizza boxes. A dented aluminum trash can, overflowing with more pizza boxes and fast-food bags, sat beside the steps to the door to what I assumed would be the kitchen.

I made my way to the door, careful not to disturb any of the trash, as much to avoid picking up some bug as to avoid noise. I mounted the steps, opposite the trash can and looked through the greasy window. The kitchen wasn't occupied, but there was an open pizza box on the counter near the sink with what appeared to be a half-eaten pizza in it, and next to it was a liter bottle of cola. A greasy bag from a local fast food outlet lay on the floor near the sink. Banner was as sloppy a housekeeper as Pearl.

I pushed on the kitchen door, expecting it to be locked. Instead, it swung inward, making a slight creaking noise. I stepped inside the kitchen and moved to the side near the refrigerator and pressed myself against it, alert for anyone who might have heard the noise of my entry, but there were no sounds.

The place smelled. It reeked of grease, sweat, and something else, like an overflowed toilet.

I made my way across the kitchen toward the opening to the interior of the house, careful not to step on anything but the kitchen tiles, which were themselves almost as greasy as the discarded fast-food bags looked. As I neared the door, the toilet smell got stronger, and there was something else mixed in with it, a coppery odor, a very familiar odor.

When I reached the opening, I stepped to my right, and then peered around the edge, keeping as much of me shielded by the wall as possible.

The room beyond the kitchen was a small dining room, with a table big enough for six, but with only four chairs. Loose, crumpled paper currency lay scattered on the table along with small plastic bags of white powder, clearly visible under the large chandelier suspended over the center of the table.

Seated in one of the chairs, facing the kitchen, was Joshua Pearl, his wide-open eyes aimed directly at me, his mouth open in a slack expression of surprise.

But, he didn't see me. He couldn't see me, or anything else for that matter. In the center of his forehead, just above his eyebrows, was a small dark hole. A small trickle of blood ran from the hole, down over the bridge of his nose, over his lips, and off the cleft in his chin. The crack of a small caliber weapon I'd heard was explained. Someone had put a round in his head. That someone had to still be in the house, but where. I felt the muscles in my back and shoulders tighten. Across from the opening where I stood, I could see the open door to the living room. I could only see a slice of it, but it looked as messy as the kitchen. Beyond that door, to the right, was another door, half open, and orange light spilled out of it.

I reached down and removed my K-Bar, thinking wryly of the old warning of not bringing a knife to a gunfight, and unsure of my next move. This was no time to play hero. I eased back into the kitchen and pulled out my phone. I hit Buster's number on speed dial, and when I answered, I quickly gave him the address, and told him about Pearl and a possible second party, Banner, with at least a small handgun. He told me to pull back and wait for the cavalry, and hung up.

His advice to wait was sound, and I was all set to do just that, when I heard the scream.

Chapter 30

It was a woman's scream, high-pitched and filled with terror. Waiting was no longer an option.

Gripping my knife, point forward and about waist high, I walked quickly to the open door. Peeking around the frame, I saw the shaky looking wooden steps leading down—I'd been right, it was the entrance to a basement.

The screaming stopped, and I heard a harsh male voice say, "Screamin' ain't gonna do you no good, so you might as well stop it."

"You have to let me out of here," a female voice said. I could hear the fear in it. "Why did you bring me here?"

"Wasn't me, it was that little turd, Josh Pearl. Said he rescued you from your mean old granddad."

"J-joshua's here? It was him that . . . I remember now, he took me from the basement at grandpa Gabe's house. W-where is he? He'll let me out of here."

"Sorry 'bout that, princess, but old Josh, he ain't gonna be doin' nothin' no more. Little fucker owed me money, and then had the nerve to pull a knife on me. Ha, I showed him. A bullet beats a knife every time. Now, here's how it's gonna be, babe. We can do it easy, or we can do it hard. Don't matter to me either way, 'cause I'm pretty hard right now. Get it, do it hard?"

"P-please, you can't do this."

"Way I see it, I can do anything I fuckin' well please, so, you either gonna cooperate, and maybe you'll even like it, or not. Don't matter one way or the other."

I heard the sound of shoes on the rough floor of the basement, and the woman's whimpering. Hoping that would cover any sounds I made, I started down the stairs, stepping on the ends of the steps to minimize squeaking. Halfway down, I paused. I could see into the basement, and was able to see a male figure, his back to me, hands at his side—and unarmed—standing over a pair of jeans-clad legs, shackled at the ankles. I was guessing the legs belonged to Lena, and the menacing hulk with his back to me was William Banner. I transferred the knife to my left hand and holding it close to my leg, resumed my downward journey.

I managed to make it to the bottom step before making a sound. That last step was so loose, it sounded like a balloon with the air rushing out.

William Banner whirled around as I stepped onto the basement floor, a look of surprise on his face. I only saw three things, in no particular order: a petite girl with hair covering her eyes, her hands taped at the wrist with duct tape and iron cuffs around her ankles, the fact that Banner needed a shave and a haircut, and the little Saturday Night Special and ten-inch blade knife stuck in his belt.

"What the fuck, dude," he said. "What you doin' in my pad. Get the fuck out of here."

He didn't go for either of his weapons, just stood there staring defiantly at me. The girl brushed the hair from her eyes and shot me a pleading look.

"Sorry, *dude*, but I'm not going to be able to do that," I said.

"Wha—"

I held my right hand up, interrupting him. "You see, I'm taking the girl with me."

A leering smile changed his already ugly, acne-scarred face into something truly macabre. The guy looked like a total psycho.

"Naw, man. You ain't takin' little Lena here nowhere. She's mine, all mine. Now, either you gonna be gone from here, or you're gonna be gone for good. You get my drift, old man?"

His attitude was beginning to chafe. I don't like being called an old man. Maybe it's because I'm becoming an old man and don't like to be reminded of it. I tried, however, not to let it show that he was getting to me. Slowly, without making any jerky moves, I eased forward, lessening the distance between us. He didn't seem to notice at first.

Then, what I was doing penetrated his drug-fogged brain. He pulled the little revolver from his belt with his left hand, and pointed it in my general direction.

"You stop right there, gramps. I know how to use this, and if you take another step, I'll put a hole in you." His smile was lascivious. "And, then I'll shoot the broad."

Of course, I stopped. Contrary to what you see on TV and in the movies, it's pretty damn hard to actually hit someone with a handgun, even at close range, and when the adrenaline is pumping, it's even harder. But, all it takes is a stray bullet, or a stroke of luck, and you've got hot lead making holes in your body. A small caliber gun like the one he held, if hits a vital organ,

Charles Ray

can kill you. If it hits an extremity, or a fleshy part of the body not covering vital organs, it hurts like hell, but won't really stop you. But, only a fool takes a chance, especially in the confined quarters we currently occupied. I wasn't close enough to reach him before he could squeeze the trigger, and running away from him was not an option, so I decided to try quiet reason.

"Look, William, or would you prefer Billy, you have to know you're not getting out of here," I said. "I've already called the cops and told them what's here, so they'll be coming loaded for bear. You wave that thing at them, and they'll turn you into Swiss cheese."

"Me and Lena will be long gone before the cops get here," he said. "All they gonna find is you and the stiff upstairs."

"And, just how far do you think you'll get? Look, kid, you're already going down for murder and kidnapping, but Maryland doesn't call for the death penalty except in exceptional cases. You kill me, and this case just got real exceptional. Give it up now, and you might catch a break."

Behind him, the girl was pushing herself upright, using the wall for balance.

"There's a dead body upstairs?" she asked when she was upright. "Who is it?"

"You don't gotta worry about it," Banner said. "Soon's I take that shit off your legs, you and me are blowin' this joint."

"The dead man's Joshua Pearl," I said. "He has a bullet hole in his head."

She stiffened, and I saw a glimmer of emotion in her eyes.

"You k-killed Joshua? He was my only friend." Her face screwed up in concentration. "I remember now. It was Joshua who took me away from the bad place. How did I end up here?"

Now, as I looked at her, her expression changed. Gone was the emotion I'd seen, replaced by . . . nothing. It was like looking at a department-store mannequin.

"I didn't have a choice, babe," Banner said. "He forced me, you see. It was him or me."

Her lips turned up in a half smile, but that smile didn't reach her eyes. They were still like two beads of colored glass.

"I understand, Billy. You did what you had to do. But, can I get out of here. I'm so tired of being tied up in this basement. I hate basements."

He smiled back at her, but kept his eyes, and the gun, on me. "You mean that? You really want to go with me? Oh hell, why'm I asking that? Of course, you do. Ain't no way you'd prefer that wuss Josh to old Billy."

"You'll take me with you? You'll let me out of this basement?"

"Of course I will, darlin'. Here, lemme just cut that tape 'round your wrists, and then I'll unlock them shackles."

He switched the pistol to his right hand, and removed the knife from his belt. It was, I could see, one of those sharp kitchen knives, the kind that comes in a set of several, and it looked familiar, but my attention was mainly focused on the little black hole at the end of the stubby barrel of the pistol that was aimed in my direction. I was, however, paying close enough attention to see the glint in Lena's eyes when she saw the knife.

She held her hands up and let him saw through the duct tape. He did it smoothly, obviously accustomed to using his left hand. I filed that away. He was holding the pistol in his off hand, so his aim, unless he was an expert marksman, which I doubted, he'd have trouble hitting a barn door, much less a moving target that just happened to be attacking him. During the fraction of a second when he was looking down at her wrists, I eased forward a step.

When the tape fell from her wrists, she stood there, leaning against him, rubbing the circulation back into them. He put the knife back in his belt and put the gun back in his left hand. I'd missed my chance, but I was almost close enough that a blitz attack just might startle him enough to make him miss, or if I was real lucky, I'd be able to kick the gun out of his hand before he could pull the trigger. Yeah, and pigs fly first class. I'd missed my chance.

I was so busy mentally beating myself up for not moving closer and faster, I almost didn't see Lena drop her hand and reach for his belt. I couldn't see what she was doing, but I could see her face, and the look she had in her eyes gave me chills. Banner now had his attention focused entirely on me, and he started to turn, to get a better aim.

He was halfway around when I saw what Lena had in her hand. He hadn't even noticed her slipping the knife from his belt. He didn't see her hand raise and then drop in a diagonal slashing motion. I doubt if he even felt it at first, it happened so fast. A bright red fountain of arterial blood spewed from his neck, drenching Lena's face and blouse, but she didn't seem to notice. His mouth opened, but the only thing that came out was a gusher of blood. His eyes went out of focus, and the hand holding the pistol trembled. His free right hand went to his throat. Before he could finish turning, and just as he was bending forward, Lena stabbed it into the center of his chest, with enough force to bury it to the hilt.

"You shouldn't have killed Joshua," she said in a monotone. "He was my friend. He was the only one who didn't think I was a bad girl."

With more strength than I would have imagined she had, she pulled the knife out. It made a quiet sucking sound as she did. Banner must've already been dead on his feet, because only a small stream of blood spurted from the wound. She sidestepped, and let his body fall forward. His head and chest hit the wall, and his body slid down until it rested face down on the floor. It had left a dark smear on the wall.

She turned to face me, the knife held loosely in her hand. Her expression was blank.

"Lena," I said quietly. "Please put the knife down. He can't hurt you anymore."

She looked down at the knife as if the hand holding it belonged to someone else.

"I am not a bad girl," she said. "I am not a bad girl."

I leaned over just far enough to slip my K-Bar back in the strap on my ankle, then I held my hands up, palms out.

"Of course, you are," I said. "And, you've been through a lot. Now, it's time to put the knife down and let me help you get out of those leg irons."

The sound of sirens, muffled and distant, but coming closer, echoed off the walls. A muscle in my jaw tensed. I took a chance, and stepped toward her.

At first, she recoiled from me, but I kept my hands in sight and kept an expression on my face halfway between pleasant and neutral. Slowly, awareness dawned in her eyes. She looked down at Banner's body and shuddered, then turned to me with a pleading look in her eyes. I motioned gently for her to drop the knife. She closed her eyes and relaxed her fingers. The knife clattered against the floor.

I stepped forward quickly and kicked it away. She just stood there, staring blankly at me.

The next part I wasn't looking forward to. The key to the manacles on her ankles was probably in Banner's pocket. I'd noticed just before she cut his throat that he'd been reaching for his right pants pocket. I walked to the corpse, knelt, and lifted the right side of his body just enough to get at the pocket on that side. The blood from the throat wound, mixed with the smaller amount from the stab wound to his chest, covered the entire right front side of his shirt, and had been absorbed by his pants, so the pocket was already dark and sticky. The coppery smell of blood, along with the smell of his evacuated bowels, was almost overpowering. I held my breath, and hoped the keys would be there.

I put on the plastic gloves, but could still feel the stickiness of the blood. I felt sharp edges and metal. A bunch of keys. I grasped them gingerly with my thumb and forefinger and pulled them out. The blood had seeped through the fabric and one of the keys, silver with a large round end, was smeared. I flipped through the keys until I saw one that looked like it might fit the lock on the manacles, a little brass key.

I knelt next to Lena, not touching her. I looked up. "I'm going to try and unlock these loops, okay?"

She stared down at me, a blank look in her eyes, for a few seconds. Then, comprehension dawned, and she bobbed her head up and down. "Yes, yes, please let me out of here. I don't like the basement. I'm not a bad girl."

She was on the verge of breaking down, and the sirens were getting louder. I carefully inserted the key, and turned. I was rewarded with a loud click, and the lock popped open. After repeating the process on the other manacle, I opened them and tossed them aside. Though freed, she stood there as if she was still tethered to the wall. I stood and gently lay a hand on her shoulder.

"Can you walk?"

"Y-yes," she said, finally seeming to be aware of my presence.

"Good, let's go upstairs. The police are coming. We can wait for them there."

She allowed me to guide her up the stairs. When we exited the basement stairwell, I blocked her view of Pearl's body, and led her to the living room.

I'd just gotten her seated on the filthy sofa when the screech of brakes, and the flashing of red and blue lights glinting through the window in the front door announced the arrival of the police.

Charles Ray

Chapter 31

When the first cop, dressed in black riot gear, broke through the front door, I was seated next to Lena on the sofa with my hands empty and in plain sight. The guy, his face obscured by a tinted plexiglass shield, was ready for action. He went into a crouch and aimed the business end of his assault rifle at my center of mass. I raised my arms in surrender, while Lena just sat there, her hands on the lap of her blood-soaked jeans, staring into space.

"Get on the floor, face down, with your hands behind your head," the cop shouted.

I was moving to comply, when Buster, wearing his armored vest, pushed in past the cop, putting a big, meaty hand on his shoulder.

"That ain't necessary," he said. "He's one of the good guys." He pointed at Lena. "I take it that's Lena Birdsong?"

"Yeah, it's her. Say, can I lower my arms?" The cop, who had been joined by four of his comrades, all looking squinty-eyed at me through their shields, looked skeptical, but Buster waved for me to lower them. "Joshua Pearl's in the next room with a bullet in his head. Banner's downstairs. He's dead, too. Throat cut and a stab wound to the chest—he's dead, too."

At the mention of dead bodies, the cops tensed. Buster seemed to take it in stride.

"You have anything to do with either of 'em?" Buster asked.

I shook my head. "Banner did Pearl," I said. "Lena here, took Banner's knife when he got too close and did him. You'll find his gun and the knife in the basement."

The county cops were now looking completely confused. Here they'd come all suited up and ready for action, and all they find is a blood-covered woman, obviously traumatized, and a black dude with no blood on him, no weapon in sight—the K-Bar was concealed by my pants leg—and two corpses to be carted off. Even though he was out of his jurisdiction, Buster took charge. He pointed at the first cop and one next to him. "You two check the basement, secure it until detectives and lab techs arrive." His big finger moved to two of the late arrivals. "You two check the next room. The rest of you, check the rest of the house."

They sprang into action as if taking orders from a DC detective was the most normal thing in the world. Buster walked over and stared down at me.

"I told you to wait for me to get here. Why don't you ever listen?"

"Honest, amigo, I was doing what you asked, but I heard a woman scream. I couldn't just stand by and do nothing."

I could see from his expression that his mind was parsing what I'd just said. I had to be inside the house to hear that scream if the woman in question was in the basement, so I hadn't really been following his instructions.

"Was Pearl already dead when you entered the house?"

"Yeah, I sound him in the dining room. I didn't touch anything in there, by the way. I went straight to the basement."

"Damn, Al, the dude had a gun, and he'd just shot someone, and you go up against him empty handed. One day your luck's gonna run out, you know that, don't you?"

Maybe, maybe not. At times like that, you do what you have to do.

"Come on. You know in my place you'd have done the same."

He grunted. "Yeah, but my 9mm would've been ahead of me goin' in. You just go in with nothin' but your bare hands."

I tapped my leg. "I wasn't exactly weaponless." My plan, had Lena not intervened by slicing Banner's throat, was to throw the K-Bar underhanded. At the distance I was from him, I wasn't likely to miss, and even if I didn't get a vital organ with the blade, the pain alone might've been enough to throw his aim off. At least, that was my plan. It might've worked, but I'll never know.

Buster just looked at me, exasperation on his face. "You still ought to get yourself a piece, man. If you're gonna keep chargin' in on dudes with guns, your K-Bar and karate chops ain't gonna cut it."

"Don't forget my feet," I said to lighten the mood.

It worked. He laughed. "Oh yeah, forgot about them deadly feet of yours."

Two of the cops he'd sent to check on the bodies came back, one from the dining room and one from the basement. The one coming from the basement looked a little pale.

"One DB in the dining room," the cop from the dining room said. "Looks like a small caliber round to the head."

The cop coming from the basement swallowed hard. "Likewise in the basement, detective. Guy's throat was slit from ear to Adam's apple. Looks like he bled out. Also got a stab wound to the chest. We found a bloody knife and a .32 caliber pistol near the body."

Both cops looked at me.

"The dead guy in the basement is William Banner. The knife and gun are both his. The stiff in the dining room is Joshua Pearl." I pointed at Lena. "One or both of them were involved in the abduction of this young woman, Lena Birdsong. She was being held in chains in the basement."

The cop from the dining room fixed me with his best official expression. "How'd she get free?" Ordinarily, uniforms don't ask questions at crime scenes when a plainclothes detective is present, but Buster was, like me, an outsider, so I gave the young cop credit for starting to gather facts to present to his own chain of command when they showed up.

"I got the key from Banner's pocket, after he was dead, and unlocked the ankle bracelets they had on her. Banner cut the duct tape on her wrists himself, just before he . . . died."

He took a small note pad and pen from his shirt pocket and began making notes. Buster stood off to the side, watching and listening, but, wisely, remaining quiet.

"How'd his throat get cut?" the cop asked. He stared at me, then turned and looked at Lena.

The blood all over the front of her blouse answered that question, but I didn't think she was in any condition to answer any questions coherently.

"After he cut her loose, he put the knife back in his belt," I said. "He was raising his weapon to shoot me, when Lena there, took the knife out of his belt and cut him. She saved my life, probably both our lives. He'd just admitted shooting Pearl, so I figure he was planning on leaving no witnesses behind."

"You had to have seen the dead guy in the dining room, and know this dude was armed," the cop said, sounding a lot like Buster. "Why in hell would you go down after him unarmed?"

"I heard her scream. I guess my reflexes kicked in and overrode my common sense."

He wrote some more, then he looked again at Lena. I could see sympathy and confusion warring for space on his face. Then, sympathy won out. He snapped his notebook shut and put it back into his pocket.

"You still took a hell of a chance," he said. "But, it probably saved her life. The detectives from Rockville station are enroute, and I called for an ambulance in addition to the coroner's van. They might have a few more questions for you, and the young lady needs to be checked by a doctor." He turned to Buster. "Lieutenant, thanks for calling us on this. As bad as it is, it could've been a whole lot worse."

Buster shrugged. "Hey, we police officers have to stick together. I'd like to think you'd do the same if you happened on something goin' down in the District."

"You can bank on it. Now, if you'll excuse me, I'm going outside to get some fresh air. This place is rank." He turned to the other officer, who still looked like he was about to be sick. "Besides, Jeff here, needs to get some air before he adds to the stink."

He clapped his colleague on the shoulder and started for the door.

"Hey," I said. "Not to tell you how to do your job, but you never asked my name. Your notes to the detectives won't be complete without that."

"Oh, I know who you are, Mr. Pennyback," he said. "We read the *Washington Post* out here, too, you know. That, and Lieutenant Mayweather told us you were the one who called him on this."

When he was gone, Buster looked at me and laughed. "Mr. Pennyback. Looks like you got yourself a fan club even out here in the burbs." His face turned serious. "Now, how 'bout tellin' me what really went down."

"It was pretty much just what I just told that young cop. I heard the shot shortly after I arrived, but I was over a block away, and couldn't be sure it came from this house. I decided to get closer and look things over after I called you. The back door wasn't locked, and I didn't hear any sounds of it being occupied, so I slipped in for a look around. I found Pearl dead in the dining room, and that was when I heard the scream. Honest, that's what happened."

"And, that tiny little thing, still chained to the wall, took out this dude with his own knife. Say, you think the Banner dude's the one that killed her grandfather?"

The evidence would support that theory. But, the evidence was, I was pretty certain, wrong. I looked at Lena, still sitting like a statue on the sofa, hugging herself and staring at nothing in particular.

"Hey, why don't we get her out front to wait for the ambulance," I said. "Sitting here, considering what she's gone through, can't be doing her much good. Maybe the fresh night air will perk her up."

He gave me a strange look, but agreed.

Charles Ray

Chapter 32

The evidence was compelling.

Lena Birdsong had been held captive in William Banner's basement, brought there, according to what Banner said, by Joshua Pearl. Pearl couldn't contradict that, him being dead and all, and killed by Banner no less. Banner's possession of the knife that was his own undoing, a knife which I felt sure the forensics techs would determine was a match for the blade that ended Gabriel Birdsong's life, would tie Banner to that crime. That, along with his demonstrated ability to take a life, his drug trafficking operation, and his threat to kill me, would be the ribbons that would tie the case up and put it in the 'closed' file.

There were, however, a few things wrong with the evidence. Things that, in their satisfaction at closing a nasty case, the police were not likely to look at closely.

I'd also closed my case. I'd found Lena Birdsong, and she was still alive, so I'd earned the fee Constance Abel was paying me. But, unlike the cops, I can't help but look at the little details. It's my nature. I'm a solver of puzzles, and there were a number of them in this case that had been nagging at my mind from day one.

An unmarked police car, still obviously a cop car because of the extra antenna and the blue light flashing on the dash, and an ambulance, arrived just as we walked out the front door. The ambulance pulled into the driveway, lights still flashing, and an EMT jumped out. He immediately took charge of Lena, walking her to the back of the ambulance, where he insisted that she lie on the gurney while he examined her. Two husky white guys in ill-fitting suits got out of the unmarked car and headed toward us. Buster moved ahead of me and had some quiet words with them. They nodded and went inside the house. He came back, and we started walking down the sidewalk until we were in front of the house next door.

I thought as we walked.

What was it about the case that bothered me?

It started with Gabriel Birdsong's body, although it didn't occur to me at the time. That realization came later, much later. Having seen Lena slice Banner's throat, though, and other things I'd noticed, but not paid that much attention to at the time, were coming to the front of my consciousness, and now, I had to decide what to do about it.

Buster stopped and held an arm across my chest.

"Okay, bro," he said. "I can tell you got something on your mind. Spill it."

"I've been thinking about this case, and there are a few things that bother me," I said.

"Such as?"

"First, there's no doubt that Banner killed Pearl, he admitted it to me. And, it's doubtful the Maryland authorities would prosecute Lena for killing him. She was his prisoner, he had a gun, and he was about to kill me. That's justifiable homicide anywhere."

"I know that, dude, but that's not what's bothering you, is it?"

This was the part I felt bad about. On the one hand, Gabriel Birdsong was bad to the bone. What he'd done to Lena was unpardonable, and in a perfect world, he would've spent the rest of his miserable life behind bars—which, given the way cons react to pedophiles, wouldn't have been long—but, murder is wrong.

"I don't think Banner killed the old man. The throat was sliced on the left side, and Banner was left handed."

"Okay, so Pearl did the old geezer, but he's dead, so case closed."

I shook my head. "I don't think so. A crime like that doesn't fit Pearl's profile. He was anti-social, I'll give you that, but, there was nothing we could find to indicate he had it in him to kill."

It took a while for it to dawn on him what I was saying.

"You're not sayin' you think—"

"Take a look at Banner's body when they bring it out, and tell me what *you* think. The cut's almost identical to the one on Birdsong, and to add to it, wasn't the old man stabbed in the chest post-mortem."

"Yeah, he was. You mean, she killed her grandfather?"

"I can't say it with any certainty, and even if she did, I'll bet a good lawyer can show extenuating circumstances. But, that knife didn't come from this house, or Pearl's house. You saw his place. Not a cooking utensil in sight. These guys lived on take-out pizza and booze. I'll bet you dollars to donuts when you check again, you'll find the knife here matches the knives in Birdsong's kitchen."

"Holy shit," he said. "I know I was lookin' at her at first, but that was because in cases like this, it's usually a family member. But, lookin' at her now." He craned his neck to look at her. She was still sitting on the back of the EMT van, a blanket around her shoulders while the EMT checked her over. "But, look at her. She's just a tiny little thing. I wouldn't even believe she did Banner if you hadn't told me."

"Well, it's just a theory, and I felt I had a duty to pass it along. What you do with it's up to you."

"Shit," he said. "I'm gonna have to think about this one. Hell, the world's probably better off without all three of 'em, and from what you found at that house, it's clear that old man put that girl through hell. Look at her. She ain't never gonna be right again."

That, I didn't disagree with. She was an adult, so she'd be pretty much on her own, unless her aunt wanted to take responsibility for her. I didn't think she'd ever be able to function in society without professional guidance, and a hell of a lot of therapy.

In some ways, being charged with her grandfather's death might be the best thing. A smart lawyer would have her undergo a psych evaluation, and I was willing to bet even the DA would as well. The result of that, I'd bet, would be a finding of not guilty by reason of insanity, and in her case, it wouldn't be a ploy. She was batshit crazy. She'd probably be spending the rest of her life in an institution with white walls, soft music, and supervised recreation sessions, which was probably best for her.

I'd done my job, but I still didn't feel good about it. But, then, feeling good about my job is not what I get paid for. I get paid for results. At the same time, as a private investigator, I have an obligation to uphold the law, not just the laws I agree with either.

Now, the ball was in Buster's court. He could just forget what I'd told him, and let the system do what the system's famous for doing—take the easy way. I didn't think he would do that, though. He's just as dedicated to doing the right thing as I am, but he also takes his oath to uphold the law seriously.

Both of us would go home, toss down a glass of something strong—vodka in my case—we'd shower, and he'd take Alma in his arms, while I would pull Sandra into a protective embrace. We wouldn't talk, just hold them close and be thankful for what we had. I couldn't speak for Buster, but I probably wouldn't sleep much. I'd just lie there all night with Sandra's warmth against my chest. He'd probably pile the twins, little Albert and Sandra, in bed with him and Alma. We would eventually talk about it, if not the next day, within a few days when time had dulled the sharp edges of the experience. We'd talk about the responsibility parents—and grandparents—have to their children, and how some people don't live up to that responsibility. The consequences aren't often as deadly as they'd been in this case, but they are devastating nonetheless, and we'd be thankful that we'd had parents and grandparents looking out for us when we were growing up. Our women would then live up to the title, significant other. They would embrace us, pat our backs, and kiss our foreheads, and they would say nothing, for they would know that at times like this, words don't do it. They would show us with their actions that they understood what we were going through, and they would always be there for us. They would be there to hold us close when we had nightmares. They wouldn't try to force us to talk about what bothered us until we were ready to talk about it. They would do what family is supposed to do.

And, the day after that, we would get out of bed, and go back to our jobs.

Books by this author:

Al Pennyback mysteries
Color Me Dead
Memorial to the Dead
Deadline
Dead, White, and Blue
A Good Day to Die
The Day the Music Died
Die, Sinner
Deadly Intentions
Death by Design
Till Death Do Us Part
Deadly Dose
Dead Man's Cove
Dead Men Don't Answer
Deadly Paradise
Kiss of Death
Death in White Satin
Death and Taxis
Deadbeat
A Deadly Wind Blows
Death Wish
Deadly Vendetta
A Time to Kill, A Time to Die
Dead Ringer
Death of Innocence
Dead Reckoning
Murder on the Menu
Over My Dead Body
Bad Girls Don't Die

The Buffalo Soldier series:
Buffalo Soldier: Trial by Fire
Buffalo Soldier: Homecoming
Buffalo Soldier: Incident at Cactus Junction
Buffalo Soldier: Peacekeepers

Buffalo Soldier: Renegade
Buffalo Soldier: Escort Duty
Buffalo Soldier: Battle at Dead Man's Gulch
Buffalo Soldier: Yosemite
Buffalo Soldier: Comanchero
Buffalo Soldier: Range War
Buffalo Soldier: Mob Justice
Buffalo Soldier: Chasing Ghosts
Buffalo Soldier: The Piano
Buffalo Soldier: Family Feud

Ed Lazenby mysteries
Butterfly Effect
Coriolis Effect
The Cat in the Hatbox

Other fiction
Angel on His Shoulder
She's No Angel
Child of the Flame
Pip's Revenge
Wallace in Underland
Further Adventures of Wallace in Underland
Dead Letter and Other Tales
The White Dragons
The Dragon's Lair
Dragon Slayer
The Last Gunfighters
The Culling
Frontier Justice: Bass Reeves, Deputy
  U.S. Marshal
Angel on His Shoulder-Revised Edition
Battle at the Galactic Junkyard
Mountain Man
Devil's Lake
Wagons West: Daniel's Journey (from Outlaws Pub.)

Nonfiction

Things I Learned from My Grandmother About Leadership and Life

Taking Charge: Effective Leadership for the Twenty-first Century

Grab the Brass ring

African Places: A Photographic Journey Through Zimbabwe and southern Africa

A Portrait of Africa

There's Always a Plan B

In the Line of Fire: American Diplomats in the Trenches

Advice for the Insecure Writer

Looking at Life Through My Lens

Ethical Dilemmas and the Practice of Diplomacy

Children's books

The Yak and the Yeti

Samantha and the Bully

Molly Learns to Share

Where is Teddy?

Catie and Mister Hop-Hop

Tommy Learns to Count

Catie Goes to School

Charles Ray

ABOUT THE AUTHOR

Charles Ray served 30 years in the Foreign Service (from 1982 to 2012), after completing a 20-year career in the U.S. Army. His first Foreign Service assignment was as a consular officer at the U.S. Consulate General in Guangzhou, China. He then served as the sole consular officer at the newly-opened consulate general in Shenyang, China, where he achieved tenure and was reassigned to the Consulate General in Chiang Mai, Thailand, as the administrative officer and acting deputy principal officer.

After three consecutive overseas tours, he returned to Washington where he served as the Special Assistant to the Director of PM Bureau's Office of Defense Trade Controls. After Washington, he went to Freetown, Sierra Leone as Deputy Chief of Mission.

In 1998, he became the first American consul general in Ho Chi Minh City, Vietnam, with consular responsibility for Vietnam from Hue to Phu Quoc Island. In 2002, he became ambassador to Cambodia, serving for three years. During the 2005-2006 academic year he served as diplomat-in-residence at the University of Houston. After leaving that job, he was appointed deputy assistant secretary of defense for Prisoners of War/Missing Personnel Affairs in the Office of the Secretary of Defense, responsible for the recovery, repatriation and identification of personnel missing from World War II to current conflicts.

His final assignment before retiring from the Foreign Service was as ambassador to Zimbabwe, from 2009 to 2012.

He holds a B.S. in business administration from Benedictine College, Atchison, KS; an M.S. in systems management from the University of Southern California; and an M.S. in national security management from the National War College. Ray is also a graduate of the U.S. Army Command and General Staff College (resident/non-resident program), the Army War College's Land Forces Commander Course, and the Defense Intelligence School's Postgraduate Intelligence Course.

His military awards include two Bronze Stars, the Joint Service Commendation Medal, Army Commendation Medal, National Defense Service Medal, Armed Forces Reserve Medal, and the Humanitarian Service Medal among others. He received a Superior Honor and a Meritorious Honor Award from the Department of State, and the Distinguished Civilian Service Award from the Department of Defense.

A native of Texas, Ray now leaves in suburban Maryland, just outside Washington, DC, with his wife, Myung.